C.J. Silverstar

Volume One:

History 101

Written By

Clayton Crawford

Published by Reilly Books
at Createspace
www.reillybooks.com

ISBN: **978-0-9919367-9-3**

Upcoming Books:

*C.J. Silverstar
Volume 2:
Extreme Metal Machine*

To learn more about
the author or his books visit:

eknakamoonknoon.weebly.com

amazon.com

smashwords.com

www.reillybooks.com

This book is dedicated to Ms. Donna Keyworth, the teacher at Charles Howitt public School who got me, a kid with ADHD, into reading, and the rest is history.

Table of Contents

The Sea of Imagination is not the visual universe, but the universe we cannot see or touch, and yet it exists in multiple dimensions and parallel worlds...

THOR'S WORLD

Without warning, like the way a lion ambushes its prey, the roar overwhelmed even me, son of Odin, the almighty Thor. I now rule a parallel world named after myself: Thor's World. I had not yet thought of a name for my new planet when the immense gravity of war pounced. My only daughter, Celestial-June, was not even three months old. My wife, Brunhild, the up-and-coming leader of the Valkyries, was taken off-guard by the sheer number of invaders: one million creatures, things like army ants falling like a torrent from an electrified ash sky!

Sif, my mother-in-law, wore the battle equipment of a Valkyrie. She walked at my left side while my wife walked on my right. We knew not our enemy's name right away. War in all of its fury had arrived at my door step.

Walking together quickly through the castle of Thor, which I personally named, but my wife told me it point blank it was a boring name and decided it should be named after our only daughter, Celestial-June. *Celestial-June's castle*, I liked it immediately. She cradled our daughter in her arms. The air flowing through the hall was unmerciful due to eroding sewage pipes damaged because the engineers had not had enough time to update the system.

I bought the new world at a good price and Brunhild liked it because it came with a castle overlooking a small lake shaped like a teardrop. She thought it would be a nice place for Celestial-June to play and swim. She convinced me to buy it from the world real estate agent. The plumbing was just one of several dozen issues that required attention. And the roof also leaks in spots. The kitchen floor contains several large pots to catch the water when it rains.

Several family members followed including several Valkyrie. They covered their noses due to the smell. I was the most fearless.

"How can you stand the stench?" Cavalier Lancelot asked. My father-in-law, Cavalier, wore the battle suit of a distinguished fire knight. I shrugged.

"We need to the engineers in this section fast," my mother-in-law recommended.

"Just as soon as we defeat the intruders, I will give the engineers that particular order, not odor," I teased.

We stepped inside a cave-like room. It contained a large egg-shaped machine with a transparent portal reminiscent of a microwave door. The large egg-shaped machine was wired up to a dozen small egg-computers along a soaring rock wall. The rock face had an engraving of the parallel universe in conjunction with several parallel galaxies and solar systems. At least the artists had had enough time to finish illustrating the wall as Brunhild requested.

"You have transformed the ceremonial hall into a madman's laboratory!" I exclaimed in shock.

"This is not something I suggested."

"Mother, no preaching, Celestial-June is new blood to the Valkyrie army and this is my choice."

"Your voice is punchy."

"And if you are not successful?" Tyr Jr. asked, the son of Tyr Sr., the god of war. He got pinged on a communication device and answered. "You have my attention," he said.

"We gain nothing if Celestial-June remains here on Thor's World," Aunt Gudrun pointed out, "Our daughter will be the last of the Valkyries."

My mother-in-law spoke up with a raspy tone, "If this ancient machine can save my granddaughter, I approve, but it is older than my brother, Odin: the winged horses are in better shape."

Brunhild decided it would be better to send Celestial-June to a parallel earth to get her out of harm's way. "It will keep my mind focussed on salvaging our world, Thor, this warrior is unlike anything we have ever witnessed," she said while placing our daughter inside the womb-like teleportation machine.

I nearly choked on a laugh while gawking at my wife's foolishness and desperation. "Sif is right; this machine is so ancient, invented before Odin's life time. What do you hope the teleportation machine will be able to do?"

"Our daughter will need a haven, a home, not this castle, not this Fortress of War," Brunhild said.

"The battlefield of Odin is receiving alien ships?" Tyr Jr. asked in a rising bewildered voice. He waited for a response from the communicator. "How many? Five hundred! This is sheer madness, create a blockage with the pegasus and seagusus. If our enemy takes Odin's battlefield the castle of Celestial, er, Fortress of War, will be left sitting helpless. Five thousand winged horses are being mounted by the Valkyrie as we speak? Excellent! Get a hold of my father, Tyr Senior, ASAP, and send a request for five thousand hammer-horsopods and three thousand horned-nosepods. Brunhild Senior is busy, my father, Tyr Senior, has a vast army of artificial-drones which can help save lives. Odin's battlefield is right on our door step!" Tyr Jr. said with a gruff voice that sounded of thinly veiled panic.

Sitting upon Tyr's shoulder, sat a bright blue and ebony coloured dingbat, twice the size of an earth owl. It released a sound akin to a wolf or dog. Tyr had a better attitude about naming things than I, the dingbat was named, Dumb-Bat.

"You are re-naming the castle? Just a moment ago you named it Celestial-June." I questioned my wife.

"A lot has happened in five minutes," Brunhild replied. She turned to her sister, Gudrun, "Have you warmed up the system?"

"I cannot imagine that it will get worse," Mother-in-Law spoke up.

"In my experience fighting battle against these creatures, I can image worse," Cavalier said. "Whoever it is attacking us, they didn't respond to our gesture of peace by accepting to play the celestial sport, hockey, which is how war should be fought; as an athletic contest, rather than barbaric bloodshed.

"The Asgardian Alfather, Odin, was introduced to hockey during the Age of Sport by a gentleman, Diefenbaker, I think is his name," I said musing. "Alfather was visiting a place on parallel Earth Two, something Canada, I think that was its name. Alfather liked to tell bedtime stories. He met Diefenbaker on a train trip across the country during a political campaign to be the leader of the political party that would give people dignity. Alfather told me Diefenbaker was a wise man and reminded him of Heimdall, the White God who protects the Rainbow Bridge," I said.

"Why did Odin go to parallel Earth Two?" Tyr Jr. asked.

"He was seeking out a new method of war, a peaceful concept of battle, but while still carrying a hammer," I said holding up my all-powerful tool.

"Hockey has become the backbone of ageless battles on ice," Tyr Jr. said, "I like the sport."

Smoke puffed out the top of one of the egg-like machines. A mechanical arm extended forward with a cone shaped instrument sucking up the smoke.

"It takes forty-eight hours," Gudrun commented and recoiled in surprise of what just happened. "One full day in our world, *de-smish*!" She swore under her breath and gave the small egg-thing a swift kick with her battle boots. It rocked back and forth. "I am teleporting Celestial-June, she will soon be on a parallel earth. Forty-eight hours to us would be estimated as one hundred and forty-eight years on that earth."

"You certainly have planned this out," I teased to cope with the stress. Odin did not believe in drugs, so medicine is forbidden as well as other forms of mind-altering stress-relieving drugs. Maybe on my world, my daughter's world, I might make an exception. "Why not simply send Celestial-June back home to live with her grandparents?" I asked.

"What?" Brunhild shrieked.

"Sorry, that is a terrible idea," I responded immediately, shaking my head. "Whatever was I thinking?"

"The last time we visited your parents, it ended in an argument about us. Need I remind you that your father did not approve of us being together," Brunhild said with a wife's *whose-side-are-you-on* tone of voice.

"I think it was his way of telling me to go seek a new world in order to build my own empire." I mused, deliberately placing a finger on my lower lip.

Tyr Jr. fed his pet a bit of food he held on his flat palm. Crumbs sprinkled the copper-stone floor. "Will Celestial-June play hockey on this earth?" he asked.

"Fate and Destiny have selected a unique path for Celestial-June, that's all they will tell me," Gudrun replied.

Brunhild closed the microwave styled door and it clicked closed with Celestial-June inside. Our daughter was comfortably wrapped inside a basket making infant sounds. She shed not a tear as I and her mother looked through the transparent window. She waved to us, apparently having fun at a crisis like this and it confirmed to me our daughter was as crazy as her mother!

Her Aunt Gudrun tugged on our sleeves to step away while she punched into the keypad a series of symbols. She was the highest level of Magisy Priest, and to work this contraption it would require her skills. With each passing symbol entered, the teleportation machine began humming more musically, gradually becoming louder and mutating sounds until it finally produced fusion music. The family members covered their ears, including me.

"The teleportation machine is so ancient, I really don't have a lot of faith in it. Will our daughter retain her natural goddess powers?" Thor asked shouting over the fusion sound.

"Arrangements for Celestial-June have been made," Gudrun said confidently and speaking loudly over the noise, "As the future queen of the Valkyries, I would not allow my only niece to go anywhere without being prepared," she added. "Instruments, and tools of the warrior trade will be supplied by Fate and Destiny."

"Fate and Destiny are extremely faithful, but they are twins that reflect both sides of the coin,"

Thor pointed out.

My wife stepped forward and her sister indicated what symbols to press and she nodded. Gudrun Jr. personally punched into keypad the last sequence of symbols and pressed the button marked: **ENTER**.

"I can see you ladies have–." I broke off in mid-sentence when something exploded with a strange sound.

Zaaa-boom!

Dumb-Bat released a loud wolf-dog sound. It jumped up off Tyr's shoulder, fluttered its wings, and then circled the room before returning and settling down. It blew out a spit of fire in tiny droplets.

"By the wings of a fire-breathing dingbat!" my mother-in-law exclaimed in shock and dismay.

The machine bucked like a stubborn creature. All the iron-grey egg-pods rocked back and forth knocking against one another. They produced the sounds of hollow drums as the fusion music faded.

All of us looked through the transparent door of the machine as Celestial-June disappeared in a splash of magical energy.

It occurred to me at that moment that I had not even had the opportunity to hold my daughter.

"Celestial-June will be re-born out of a selected woman on a parallel earth," Aunt Gudrun said. "The woman that Fate and Destiny selected bares the maiden name Valkyrie, and her entire clan has a distinct bloodline of heroines, employed through the Atlas Corporation Care Division of nurses."

"Alfather has told me about the Atlas Corporation, in more bedtime stories than I can remember. It was the first leaf-world on the farther tip of the highest branch of the Ash World Tree closet to the pool of celestial milk which drips life into our world," I said always intrigued at my father's knowledge. "The Atlas Corporation provides medical training as well other nurturing education to All-Worlds on the Yggsdrasil Tree. The Moonsteep race was born from the Emmaga People, the ones who originated before Cronus and Alfather," I continued priding myself on learning from Odin.

Gudrun continued, "My niece will learn nursing skills. And the father originates from the Silverstar clan and they produce a bloodline of soldiers and wealth, both military and industrial. My niece will learn both nursing skills and battle skills. She will become a Valkyrie on earth."

"Have mercy on mortal men," I joked. "Gudrun, you have always proven to be a wizard," I said, "You studied under Zerlin, father of Berlin, who fathered Merlin. Hope is in my heart."

"Hope is all we have," Tyr Jr. said.

Boom! Boom!

"Our enemy is blasting energy bolts at the Castle of Celestial-June!" One of the palace guards announced rushing inside the Womb-Teleportation Machine room .a.k.a. the former ceremonial room. I thought about correcting him on the new name of the fortress, but let the subject drop.

"To battle!" Sif exclaimed. My mother-in-law as the current Queen Valkyrie would never back down from a battle, just like myself. We got along famously.

The war on the Fortress of War raged and on the day it ended, my finest soldiers were defeated. Brunhild and I sent a final message to Celestial-June before being captured by multi-limb purple coloured creatures. I found my arms pinned at my sides.

A fire knight attempted to rescue us, but just one of those purple creatures captured him and tore his arms out of their sockets. His head was spun around and his neck gruesomely broken.

We were brought face to face with our enemy and put on our knees. The leader radiated with a cosmic energy of dark blue, eyes glowing all-white.

The Fortress of War exploded because Gudrun had placed explosives throughout to prevent our enemy from capturing any advanced Odin technology, but Dr. Methopolis already possessed a wealth of technology.

Our enemy finally reined in his supernatural powers. "I am a Bluelaser, a person from Moonsteep," he said as his hand flicked out in a blur.

I was left powerless as a tiny dart pricked my skin and injecting a formula he invented. "I am not from this parallel world, Thor, so your god-like abilities can be supressed. I am native to Moonsteep, and we pride ourselves as being the surgeons of the ocean of space. There is nothing you can do with your god-like powers that I or my people cannot figure out through science and use it to our advantage. Unfortunately, many of my people consider me a criminal and insane," he said offhandedly, "but they are merely disgruntled at my sheer will power and genius," he added while injecting a black formula under my skin.

A staff of nurses followed his commands and injected thousands of my people with this black serum that demonstrated his power over our inner anatomy. My wife looked at me helplessly as she was also injected with this formula.

"Does my enemy have a first name?"

"Dr. Methopolis will suffice."

And then we were put in a prison camp and forced to slave labor for this Dr. Methopolis. All I had to hang onto were my lonely thoughts, and a dim sense of hope for the future.

Celestial-June, my only daughter, she is the last of Valkyries.

CAMERON KNIGHT NEWSPAPER

QUEEN-KNIGHT WEEK EDITION EST. 1867
(Excerpt from the Sports section, date unknown)

The Queen-Knights junior team has been shaking up the Atlas Corporation Hockey co-ed League (ACHL). The players include: Susan a.k.a. Captain Determination (a Sumerian – centre), Fazillah a.k.a. The General (a Sumerian – left wing), C.J. Silverstar a.k.a. the Valkyrie (a Sumerian - right wing), Zack (a Murian – left defense), Timothy a.k.a. the Shark (a Sumerian – right defense) and Christina Tereshkova a.k.a. (a Murian – left wing), Skylar a.k.a. (a Murian – right defense) Tiger-Girl (a Sumerian – goalie) – these names are the names of those who are now considered by Youth Hockey Canada (YHC) as the dream-players.

When the Queen-Knights hit the ice, from face-off to final goal, the action never ceases.

It is the first time in hockey history that so many Sumerians and Murians have been on a single team.

The Sumerians, with the likes of C.J. Silverstar, can actually keep up with the supernatural Murians scoring as many as 50 goals in 2043 and again in 2044. Currently in 2045, she has scored 95 goals smashing a record set by hockey player Brainne Jenner in 2020 at the tender of age of twenty. C.J. is eighteen and has a remarkable acrobatic-like skill on the ice. C.J. will always be remembered as the girl who at sixteen, actually performed a cartwheel on the ice and landed back on the blades of steel while deeking out two opponents. Jenner scored 80 goals over an entire season including her time in the play-offs, while C.J. has accomplished 90 goals with three more games to play in the regular season. The championships in Hockey City will commence on June 3rd 2045. The sports world has dubbed C.J., the Valkyrie on ice, but she is not the captain, that title belongs to Susan Lemieux.

Skylar, from the same team, has managed to score fifty goals although he possesses supernatural powers as all First World people do. It is written in the rules of ACHL that though they possess extra abilities, they don't show off or use them to take advantage at a game. The Murian People strive to ensure their kids obey the laws and don't brag of their talent. Skylar can be viewed as a boy that could shake-up the NHL, but because of his supernatural ability might be subject to scrutiny. On several occasions when NHL players have admitted to being Murians, they have been fired and sued by the league, three such infamous law suits occurred during the twentieth century. It is considered cheating not to include clauses for the extra abilities in their contracts.

However, the ACHL rules encourage Murians to explore their powers and trust the players to keep them in check. Heck, all kids should be allowed to play hockey because this is the Canadian sport religion!

CAMERON KNIGHT NEWSPAPER

QUEEN-KNIGHT WEEK EDITION EST. 1867
(Excerpt from a Medical Article, Date unknown)

Earth's First World Race, the Murians, are experiencing an incline of a peculiar illness unlike anything they claim has ever happened in their five hundred thousand year history on this planet. Medical officials of the World Health Organization, representing the Murian people, the W.H.O.-Murian Medical Society (W.H.O.-M.M.S.), are puzzled why twenty-five thousand are so weak they can no longer utilize their supernatural gifts. They are not yet prepared to claim this is a pandemic.

Symptoms typically include a swelling headache, five to eight small chicken-pox-like bulbs on the left or right temple, pale eyes that differ from the natural opaque pupil-look that shift to a pale green sickly colour. Other medical exams have shown the addition of dark brown smudges. No inoculation is issued, but is being pursued by doctors at the Canadian research facility in Saskacity, which also has instruments for measuring a level five virus like Ebola.

Since 2014 W.H.O. has issued a report there are now seven known super-bacteria to be aware of, escherichia coli, klesbsilla pneumonia, methicillin-resistant nontyphoidal salmonella, shigella, and neisseria gonorrhoea: these are current drug resistant bacteria, but lately the Atlas Corporation has provided a serum defeating the symptoms of escherichia coli and shigella, though it is not a cure. This new type of bacteria causing the outbreak is being called by doctors Moonsteep Bacteria, because we are in the space age and apparently W.H.O. has a sense of humor after all these years. It could be extra-terrestrial, but W.H.O. is not going to imply that possibility right away. Although many Mars colonists have returned home, they are given full medical treatment before returning to Earth.

Good news has been announced for the W.H.O.-M.M.S.; the CEO of Atlas Corporation, Mr. Cee-Dee Seven, has offered the corporations vast medical services to aid the First World race at minimum cost. In a statement released, CEO Mr. Seven said, "There has come a curious situation involving the Murian people. They are a gift to this earth, because they claim their procurators, the Annunaki, arrived here long ago. This implies they originated from another world, not from outer space, but between the spaces of worlds and universes, a parallel dimension. Go ahead and chuckle, but as farfetched as it sounds, we now possess an international space station, a moon base and a colony on Mars with seven thousand humans. What if people from earth were to arrive on another world as we did with Mars, and so we would father a new civilization on that world. Or if we were to arrive at another populated world within our own Milky Way Galaxy, we would be guests. Let's be friends: three important words, just as important as when a man says to a woman, "I love you". Together we will help our friends, the Murians. There are a mere estimated seven million living today."

CEO Cee-Dee Seven has helped steer governments around the world by providing medical aid and education. It is known as the good-guy company, the Atlas Corporation, and it has been active in wars around the world providing platoons of street surgeons and aiding the sick and wounded. On Doomsday 6th June 1944, the Atlas Corporation provided a three thousand Street Surgeons, but where on earth they originated from remains a mystery. No one bothered to argue during Doomsday, the allied forces simply wanted to overthrow the Nazis and the code name for the invasion was: Overlord.

In 1960, Prime Minister John Diefenbaker announced to the world assembly of nations that Murians in Canada would no longer require a living-passport to reside here, and made them all citizens. By 1967 the United States followed, as did Great Britain, but other countries still regulate and insist the Murians require a living-passport.

The Murian Island off the coast of Denmark, is the official island where a small Murian Nation was set up in 1939, with an estimated five hundred thousand occupants. It has not yet been officially recognized as a country, but in 2025 it did receive a winning vote in a pact that stated that no country would invade it or try to steal it away as the Nazis once attempted. Germany made the official vote and gave it a certificate of approval.

C.J.'S BLOG
(SilverNorth@HaHa.ca)

Welcome to my blog, it is not for the normal person, but who on Earth is normal anyway? Normal scares me to death.

With great thanks to the guidance from the Atlas Corporation HQ in Metroburb, humanity has achieved incredible events; the donut International Space Station (ISS) with a population of one thousand in 1975; a moon base with a population of 5,000 by 2003; and the Mars colony with a population of 3,000. The most senior and most powerful corporation has helped humanity in way no normal corporation could possibly imagine.

But still, with all our achievements there is homelessness and extreme poverty, and sporadic wars and I have come to the conclusion is part of the human equation. Although the former Prime Minister helped achieve peace in Vietnam through the Canadian "Open Skies Peace Program", in 1966 using our Arrows as the instrument of protection and sending in 2,500 Canadian soldiers as peacekeepers, the America politics shifted to the aggressive Chinese. The two armies clashed for two and a half years, ending officially on the 20th of September, 1969.

The Americans managed to keep the Chinese military out of Vietnam, although they were outmanned eight to one. In terms of ground combat the Americas fought toe-to-toe with everything they could muster, demonstrating to the globe how they could sink their teeth into an enemy. One hundred thousand Americans served in this toothy, snarling and hot jungle battle: ten thousand soldiers died before the end arrived. The Americas, along with a handful of First World Murians, disabled China's heavy water factories and prevented the manufacturing of atomic bombs. They decided to officially end the conflict for good, and just as Americans prevailed over Japan, they dropped atomic bombs: one on 11th September 1969, over Beijing, and a second one over Shanghai on the 14th of September, despite warnings and posturing from Moscow. In the end, Moscow did not in fact engage the Americans with nuclear missiles as previously warned.

"Whew!"

The Berlin Wall crumbled an estimated eighty-six years ago and Germany became unified. The president of Russia, Gorbachev is the dude who let the east re-unite. But, he admitted in an interview to a TV journalist in Canada, "The Russian council discussed retaliation against the U.S.'s atomic droppings of bombs on China for forty-eight hours. Poor Beijing and Shanghai. Canada got in the middle and it generally felt there was no need to send our missiles over Canadian airspace just in case one might detonate over Metroburb or even Ottawa.

Canadians have always been peacekeepers; the Vietnam Open-Skies program by former Prime Minister Diefenbaker, is one example. The Canadian military even protected Russian's northern territory, Siberia, during a skirmish, the secret unofficial Artic Battle…I won't comment about the Artic Battle for national security reasons as our nations are friendly."

With extreme wealth there is extreme poverty, like a magnet, one is north and the other is south. And to combat this unbalance in humanity one must make a choice, life is about choices: I learned that from my parents by the age of twelve.

"Whew!"

My Mom's family name is Valkyrie, and during every major war that Canada was involved in; the first, the second, Korea, Vietnam, the Gulf War and Afghanistan conflict, three relatives got involved.

My Mom's cousin, a special person in many ways, so my mom tells me, Aunt Gudrun, would not allow fear to control her emotions. She was a Canadian Lieutenant in Afghanistan, a nurse who worked in the battle-field as a Medic. I never really knew Aunt Gudrun, except through oral stories told to me at my bedside by my mom.

Aunt Gudrun gave my mom two gifts: one was a paperback book containing battle illustrations of oddball dressed people like from another parallel world. The title: the Valkyries. The second gift was a small marble which glowed blue.

"Weird or what?"

During a nature walk at the age of twelve, on a primary school field trip, I slipped off the wooden boardwalk. I landed in a cesspool of gunk, not ordinary mud because it glittered with an exotic slime. Fumes rising from the gunk put me to sleep... At times I don't want to remember the episode, but other times I get flashbacks of faces... "What has happened to me?" And a voice answered me, "I am your father, I am Thor, son of Odin, you are my daughter, C.J., and this is your true mother, Brunhild. Your real name is Celestial-June."

The world around me spun, I thought I would pass out, but everything stopped as if I was somehow teleported to a state of tranquility. It was magical.

Brunhild spoke to me, while the holographic parents held my nervous shaking hands, "We cannot be here for long, it's a long distance mind-up-link, expensive, but we connect to your mind through our Dream-Machine communication system. I can tell you this much, the soil you fell into is from Thor's World and it contains an adapting organism, which will not harm you and will not affect Sumerians or Murians of parallel earth number two, but it will however infect your cells giving you unlimited fantastic powers far beyond the Murians, possessing nearly the identical strength as an Annunaki person. Use your powers to fight battles wisely; I do not want to be preachy."

Thor stepped closer to me as a hologram, "I cannot embrace you in this manner of communication, but I wish I could, my only daughter."

"Weird or what?"

I shared what I saw with no one. If my parents learned about this episode they might think I had gone mad, insane or off-my-rocker. Pick one, and then it would be right time to call in the guys in the white suits and fit me a stylish straight jacket. As far as I know, straight-jackets go over big inside institutions with white walls and the only voice inside your head is your mind going nutty. I am a teenager close to graduating from Queen-Knight High School, and that's not where I would like to spend my adult life: being the hamster for some mad scientist. It's the mad scientist who should be inside the institution with his head wired up to an EKG like some sort of evil and twisted Merlin. Don't forget the cone hat made of tinfoil.

Newspapers keep me informed of what goes on in this world and sometimes people commit suicide inside institutions, driven to sheer madness because they are treated as creatures rather than as people and are always drugged up.

My father is RCMP Sgt. Gary Silverstar, and my mom is a street nurse employed by the Atlas Corporation Global Care Giver Division. My parents are superheroes in their unique careers. They suspect something traumatic occurred to me at the Metroburb Science Centre, but that is not what happened, they have no idea of the truth. Though I have no proof to back up my beliefs of what happened that day, I am extremely confident that I am not mad.

I don't know if Thor or Brunhild will return to speak to me, but I hope to one day be reunited with them again. I have so many questions, and they seem to be the only ones with the answers.

I keep the use of my power to a minimum, but it is difficult when people are in need of someone to fight for them so they won't be picked on.

"Oh, oh, just a second, here is something for my blog!" *Laughing to myself!*

Sandy May Lu, my good friend, is an escort although she attends Queen-Knight High School to complete her education. This is how she supports herself because her parents kicked her out at sixteen after discovering she was a lesbian. The story goes Sandy's parents found her in her bedroom with a girl dressed as a guy and they were in teenage love. Sandy May Lu lives with two other girls.

A balding pot-bellied guy of maybe two hundred and seventy pounds, was bothering Sandy May Lu one day at the Valkyrie Diner, (it's owned by my mother's side of family and located inside the Valkyrie Hotel on Sir John A. Macdonald Avenue), anyway, the guy would not leave her alone. He was a class A dick. His jokes were rather stupid to say the least. I witnessed all this while waitressing part time, so I approached the customer and asked him kindly to stop. Instead, he focussed his attention on me, giving my butt a squeeze, so I punched him the nose and it popped red.

Chad, my boyfriend, leaped to his feet a second later. He put up his fists in the traditional boxer's pose, ready to defend me. (He took boxing because he played rough and tumble hockey, but he was not a hockey goon). Chad didn't take shit though.

Hockey buddies from the Thunder-Screamers quickly assembled from the surrounding booths, to help just in case he required back up. However, Chad stood six foot and three inches and I knew he weighed a solid two hundred and forty pounds, he was built like a five tonne truck.

A pair of tall, rock solid Queen-Knight RCMP officers entered the Valkyrie Diner as if on cue. The police wasted little time; one took my statement, and the other broke up the crowd and slapped the handcuffs on the potbellied customer.

"You're my hero!" Sandy May Lu squealed in a gush. She jumped out of the booth and with her girlfriends and customers looking on; I received a hug from the three girls. People laughed. Chad laughed. The teammates of the all-boys' hockey Triple-A team laughed. The guys applauded me. I'm not going to lie, It felt good.

Chad gave me a kiss. "Next, time, I will bounce the next asshole out of this diner."

"Do nothing of the sort, young man," the black Queen-Knight RCMP officer instructed. "If you get an arrest record, it could affect you if you go pro in hockey, Mr. Westwind," he added.

"I will take out the trash," the other RCMP Officer said.

"Friggin' towel head!" Potbelly cursed.

The Muslim RCMP Officer replied with a cheesy smile, "Actually, this is a turban. Don't sweat it; you will have plenty of time learning to spell T-U-R-B-A-N."

The two Queen-Knight RCMP officers took the class A dick away.

End of Blog No. 1925

CAMERON KNIGHT NEWSPAPER

QUEEN-KNIGHT WEEK EDITION EST. 1867
(Excerpt from the Crime Section, date unknown)

The RCMP is speaking to witnesses in the city of Britannia about a person wearing a cloak. Witnesses that have spoken to reporters claim it bears an emblem, but the police's mouths are locked shut on the subject. RCMP Sgt. Silverstar is in charge.

Witnesses tell Metroburb reporters that the cloaked person interceded into the middle of a brawl between two known Britannia street gangs: the Thugs and Hoods.

Zoom!

The cloaked person singlehandedly battled the gathered Thugs and Hoods, breaking up the street brawl by performing lightning quick martial art moves mixed with fantastic gymnastics. Twelve young men all of them under the age of eighteen, the youngest being thirteen, were knocked about like ragdolls, but no blows were life threatening. The boys received mostly bruises, but some received a broken arm or wrist.

Several homeless people were protected by the cloaked person during the fight.

And for our Metroburb two hundred and thirty thousand daily readers: this crime situation involving the cloaked person is not to be confused with the mysterious Street Surgeon. The cloaked person demonstrated a power only a Murian could possess.

A spokesperson for the local First World from the Murian Enclave, tucked inside the town of Queen-Knight, spoke on this matter: "None of our citizens would be so foolish, but there are some brats locked away inside the Saskacity Murian Supermax. We teach our supernatural children a superhero must first receive a license from the Government of Canada."

Terry Savage, the leader of Canada's elite superhero agency, H.O.C.K.E.Y., will not comment on the situation of Britannia being tight-lipped.

CEO Gilbert Canoe of Britannia's super five companies nicknamed The Hand, made this comment on the matter, "We hope the RCMP captures the cloaked figure and brings that person to face judgement, otherwise, whoever that person is, man or woman, will one day be injured, perhaps by one of several gangs lurking within Britannia."

C.J. AND CHAD'S FLIGHT

C.J. sat behind the wheel of her Cessna she had nicknamed Silver-Bird. There were definitely perks to having a rich uncle. Through the windshield she could see the runway becoming shorter and shorter and straight ahead was the thick Richardson Forest. Chad cast an expression at her.

"You want to fly or crash?" he asked.

C.J. giggled. She gently pulled back on the H-shaped wheel and Silver-Bird responded lifting smoothly off the runway. It flew over the thick Richard Forest, a part of a well-groomed estate complete with a golf course. The forest was merely a clump left alone to provide protection and privacy.

"Chad, while I am navigating Silver-Bird, read your history report, I would like to listen," she said and deliberately placed a hand on his chin, turning his head to gaze into his eye.

"Is there something wrong?" he asked curiously.

"Nothing, sorry," C.J. replied, stretching the word as she felt her heart skip two beats. Immediately she turned her attention to the controls, her eyes flicking here and there as she read the panel of flight instruments.

"I know Mr. Beerdeer won't exempt me from reading aloud, I'm just not that lucky," Chad said and shared a chuckle with her. He lifted his red and purple knapsack which had pins clipped with various yesteryear rock faces including the new Canadian group called the Super Assassins. Some pins were faces of past hockey stars, one of them Phil Esposito, Captain of the 1972 all-Canadian Team that played against the Russian Red Machine.

"Britannia", Chase began, stopping long enough to clear his throat. "When the fathers of confederation created Canada as a country in 1867, they also invented a unique situation in Lower Canada within an area seventy-five kilometers from York (Toronto), and one hundred and fifty kilometers east of Metroburb. They wanted a city which would be a tax haven and thus Britannia was born in 1870, after some legal wrangling with the Canoe family and a large sum of money paid to the Canoe Clan.

Originally the area designated to become Britannia consisted of twelve farms and covered approximately twenty-five kilometers in area. All the farms belonged to the Canoe Clan, one hundred and fifty members belonging to a unique religious group, Christian Farming Merchants. Other than farming and trading with other communities at farmer markets, building canoes was one other business the Christian Merchants were involved in. They had settled in the area in the year 1735 and quickly established control over the region running smaller farms.

Between 1737 and 1745 the Christian Merchants waged a war on the souls of men and women who they accused of witch craft. There were beheadings by guillotines, simple hangings, and in other situations drownings. They hunted down the First World Murians, and using the Bible as a weapon, stirred up a storm of fury with the local non-supernatural people who engaged in supernatural spiritual inflammatory methods. Murians could have easily defeated the Christian bigots, but they felt it was wrong to use their powers in case it provoked hatred. Five Murian families agreed to pack up the wagons and leave without incident in 1745. The Canoe Clan now owned the entire region.

Early fur traders such as Mr. Lawrence and explorers such as the Mackenzie Clan required equipment for enduring the harsh Canadian north. The Christian Farming Merchants made an economic pack with many explorers. This included building a ship called the Annandada for Captain James Cook, founder of Australia, so he could sail through the northern portion of the Artic. The Christian Farming Merchants were in direct competition with the North West Company.

Alexander Mackenzie, one of Canada's greatest northern explorers, discovered the Beaufort Sea. He also found the Mackenzie River.

Britannia was born in 1870. The Christian Merchants decided to immediately take their government expenditures, making investments in several companies. One of the companies was a coffee plantation in Brazil, the dark liquid every man craves for a boost; and while in South America,

Columbia, they also invested farming community growing marijuana to harvest Hemp clothes. In the United States, they invested in a small company in western Pennsylvania and captured a niche in the fuel avenue. Another investment was in a soft drink company called, Soda-Pop, created by a German scientist, Dr. Meth and it had quickly entered the North American market in 1888. It set up the head office in Metroburb, the city south of Queen-Knight. They made agreements to each company to handle the economics all across Canada because the Christian Merchants owned the local bank Canoe Economic Services (CES). In total, their government investments ranged around five million dollars.

Their iron-grip on Britannia in the beginning always enforced shutting down business on Sundays, sticking to Christian beliefs, but all that changed by 1901 as the nature of business changed.

The Christian Merchants began developing a plan to take all twelve farms and transform them into as a city under the name Britannia. The Canadian Government gave them a green light under the arrangement that it would be protected as a tax heaven.

In the beginning of construction, when equipment and tools were purchased with profits from investments, it was ragtag. There was also wrangling between the families as some of them were losing faith in the idea of building a tax free city. Although they had good earnings from share profits in those various companies, some family members were not sure if building the city was such a great idea, but just as the families were about to splinter, two catastrophes occurred that saved the Christian Merchants including the CES. The second, was the beginning of the Great War, the devastating World War I.

However, prior to the declaration of war in 1914, was the cataclysmic sinking of the H.M.S. Titanic in April of 1912. The strangest thing occurred, as if by cosmic coincidence, the six heads of the Christian Merchant Clan were aboard the Titanic for its maiden voyage, and they died as a result. The entire Clan was placed on the shoulders of their sons, but they were no match for one family member, a charismatic man, Gilbert Boulderfellow. The family members wore traditional cloaks bearing Christian symbols, yet Gilbert's was a little different. He often wore a cloak with strange symbols, and when Gilbert spoke he seemed to possess the ability to hypnotize people with mere words. Unbeknownst to them, it had been taken from the long ago Moonsteep race that lived in ancient Greece.

Under the leadership of Gilbert, the other Clan members simply let him speak to the Canadian Government in parliament as their representative. As war waged across the globe, he cast a powerful hypnotizing voice and the members agreed to allow Britannia to build large warehouses to help manufacture weaponry and other military equipment.

Gilbert decided to start five companies as a direct business enterprise; Beaver, for marine enterprises, the Moose Construction Company, The Loon Company that developed flight equipment, the Polar Bear Company for cold weather pursuits, and the Mallard Company that handled wildcard requirements. In the centre of those companies was the CES bank. They employed as many as one hundred thousand Canadians during the war era, the largest body of employment compared to the twenty-five thousand working in Metroburb City.

The five companies also competed with the Silverstar Clan in Scotland during the Great War. The Silverstar military-industrial family HQ was located in Metroburb and the captured the market providing engines for British ships and aircrafts. It gained a reputation because of the engines built for the two British ships during the war of 1812, H.M.S. Scotland and H.M.S. Silverstar.

During the years of the Great War, the people working in the warehouses required somewhere to live and so an inner city zone was designed and simply called, The Living Zone. It was The Living Zone in which they lived, shopped for needs, and it had a single school, a single church and park area.

Twenty-one Murian families with supernatural powers lived there among the Sumerian mortals since the Great War began, but by 1929, six families had moved out, leaving only fifteen. They did not want to raise their offspring in an environment without green, without soaring trees, and no way to touch soft leaves in the summer and crumple dry leaves in the fall season. They wanted to see their kids playing in piles of leaves, as Murian games included making piles and jumping into them. The idea would later catch on with Sumerian families. They wanted the odor of a farming community, and the Murian Enclave was the perfect spot for them to go to raise a family. The only odor they could smell now was concrete and steel, and the burning of coal spewing from soaring super chimneys.

By the end of the Great War, Gilbert had persuaded the Christian Merchant Clan to agree that the city of Britannia would not include any schools, churches, hospitals, parks or trees. It would be dedicated to business. In 1921, he borrowed millions of dollars from U.S. barons and ordered construction on five skyscrapers, each one two hundred and fifty meters tall and a one hundred meter building in the dead centre that was to become CES Ltd. He personally came up with a new name for the five skyscrapers, The Ring of Fire, although some family members were irked by the idea, but they could not overrule Gilbert. The roaring twenties gave way to new business ventures.

The Moose Construction Company began digging the holes. Many of those first families who lived in Britannia during the Great War became the source for the next phase. They were given shares of the Ring of Fire.

The Sumerian families expanded and the single school became overcrowded, but no further schools were built. The Ring of Fire refused to spread their wealth into building any new schools and so students were shipped out by a single Christian Merchant family, the Noah Horse-Bus Company to Scarborough schools and far away Toronto. Scarborough was an estimated twelve kilometers east of Britannia. The Noah Horse-Bus Company refused to charge the Sumerian Families the cost of transportation. Some Sumerian families simply began educating their kids at home, and their education began fall behind students in Upper Canada, Montreal and Lower Canada, as well as the Toronto region.

The fifteen Murian families remaining in the Living Zone began to help the Sumerian Mortals because they needed food during the dirty thirties. The Ring of Fire refused to set up soup kitchens ignoring its Christian roots. However, the Noah family aligned itself with Earth's First World, agreeing that forcing people to work and only providing means to feed them was evil.

When Noah was approached by Gilbert on the only farm still untouched and challenged for providing services without charging a price, a proposition was made. "The Christian Merchants, and the Ring of Fire will not allow a Clan member to disturb the economic system we have set up in Britannia. This is our tax haven, what gives you the right to do things differently?"

Noah merely explained, "God doesn't charge me to plant seeds on his soil, to farm it for food, or to feed my family, and if he allows food to grow in abundance then why should I charge another family? If I choose take their kids to another location so they can receive an education this God's will."

Noah was judged by the Merchant CEOs, accused of witchcraft and aligning his family with the supernatural families, the Murians. In 1930, was hanged for his crimes outside a dilapidated church. The single church, once built in 1914, was now weathered, with splinters in the wooden roof and cracks in the floor. It had been as forgotten as the religion it had once stood for.

Sumerian families which harnessed the Fire of Ring business attitude were given special status in the community and were given new homes in the single high rise apartment complex.

Those five businesses were completed in September 1929, a week before the collapse of Wall Street. There are claims that Wall Street barons demanded the Ring of Fire pay back in full all of the borrowed money, which could have avoided the stock market crash of 1929, but it refused, adhering to the contracts signed by those barons and Gilbert Boulderfellow could not be legally arrested. He beat the barons at their own slick financial game and simultaneously was the cause of the dirty thirties. Gilbert did not seem to mind being labeled as the black sheep by American businessmen, and the

Christian Merchants families accepted him as their hero. The Ring of Fire survived the 1929 crash which in the United States, caused some five thousand banks to be annihilated and like some virus, spread out to as many as sixteen thousand banks. Meanwhile, the Ring of Fire had an abundance of cash on hand left over from their initial borrowings. It also had three thousand gold bars obtained through illegal activity, and stored in the vaults securing it even more on economic terms. The U.S. and the global economy fell into the first twentieth century depression.

Gilbert decided to fly to Germany in 1930 on a strange mission as he told the family members. He had to meet a young German man that would change the world forever. What was odd about Gilbert is while other family members aged over the years, he never seemed to. He disappeared from the Christian Merchant Clan leaving a will for his only son to be the heir of the empire if he should never return from Europe.

"Gilbert Canoe is now the current head honcho of Britannia's five super companies nicknamed, The Hand," Chad concluded.

"Well done." C.J. replied after listening for one hour. She adjusted the wheel, turning Silver-Bird to circle a northern city with a population of one hundred thousand.

"Hockey City, you're circling Hockey City!" Chad exclaimed, recognizing the only fifty storey skyscraper within three hundred kilometers. It dwarfed the five smaller buildings surrounding it, putting it in the centre, making it number six. It wasn't a coincidence that hockey is played with six players: the captain typically at centre, the left wing and right wing players, two defensemen and the goalie. The smaller buildings were no taller than ten stories. The upper portion of the famous skyscraper displayed two tall glowing hockey sticks that crossed over one another under on an electronic flashing sign displaying the name: HOCKEY CITY.

"The Queen-Knights play a ramble-rustle tournament versus the Saskacity Antiflick-Troopers this Friday, so I need to know now, will you be in attendance, Chad?" C.J. veered away from Hockey-City.

"It's a quintessential game; two hockey games back-to-back, with only a three hour intermission. I would not dream of missing the action."

"Punishment is your ally in hockey," C.J. replied with a no nonsense tone.

"You're the one to speak about punishment because you're the one who enjoys spending entire nights wandering through Britannia," Chad commented.

"The winner of this three-game ACHL tournament gets to play the Metroburb Stanley Cup winners for the bi-annual charity game viewed by nearly three billion TV viewers," C.J. commented ignoring his previous remark.

"May 21st, 2045," Chad said. "Have you ever

met the mysterious Street Surgeon?" he asked.

"Ebony Shine is my personal business," C.J. replied navigating the Silver-Bird back home to Queen-Knight.

THE ISLAND OF STABILITY

Thunder exploded as the storm produced multiple forks of shimmering lightning and cloud-to-cloud electrical energy. It was a perpetual storm of the apocalyptic kind.

Under the warring electrical clashes, resisting high winds capable of tearing apart human flesh, the fortress was moulded straight out of the copper-red rock. A supernatural energy dome acted as an umbrella protecting it from the savage storm.

"Dr. Methopolis, your plans were executed where the Viking god lived. Thor and his family were captured, it was masterfully planned, congratulations," Number Three said.

Standing in a circular room surrounded by five wall sized HDTV monitors, Dr. Cronus Methopolis stood. He wore a traditional Moonsteep cape-coat worn by only those who were born as Bluelaser people, but instead of the bright blue one, his midnight blue cape set him apart. The collar was typically raised. He smoked one of those long-pen cigarette holders. The gizmo gave him a sweet taste when he puffed.

"Extracting precious minerals from parallel planet 0009834732-QK will certainly bring Balderdash a guaranteed income," Number Eight spoke up and released a giggle for pleasure.

"Money is not my primary goal," Dr.

Methopolis replied.

"Bluelaser People of Moonsteep are blind when it comes to commerce," Number Twelve said.

"I am aiming my next target at a parallel Earth," Dr. Methopolis stated, "as Project Leader is aware." He puffed on the smoke-gizmo.

"What do you mean? Explain, Project Leader!" Number Three insisted. On the screen he was chewing on a sandwich full of squirming things.

Project Leader cleared his voice, "Ahem." The microphone squealed a couple of times. He continued. "Dr. Methopolis and I have decided to advance forward now that world 0009834732-QK is under our direct control. A parallel Earth has come to our attention located in the Xavier Zone in the Pinwheel Parallel Universe Map."

At that moment a colourful transparent hologram map appeared in the circular room. Dr. Methopolis stood in the centre. It showed thousands of parallel worlds in relationship to dozens of different dimensions and multiple universes simultaneously. He pointed a remote control and pressed a button zooming in on the particular area.

A hologram comet went zooming by and it looked as though it smacked Dr. Methopolis upside the head and exploded on impact.

"Dr. Methopolis learned of this parallel earth by using potent mind serum to extract information from Gudrun, the Magisy god in the Viking world," Project Leader said and continued, "Together Dr.

Methopolis and I have already fractured the economy of this world time after time, as well as penetrating dozens of their secret societies including the Bilderbergs."

"We are Balderdash and this parallel earth has a group called, Bilderbergs," Number Twelve said, "how poetic," he added.

"The Bilderbergs are the strongest force of economics on this parallel Earth as far we can tell, and it is comprised of twelve families, but rumors exist of a thirteenth family," Dr. Methopolis said.

"Project Leader, what have you accomplished?" Number Eight asked impatiently.

"Are the armies of this parallel earth capable of withstanding an assault?" Number Seven asked speaking up.

"Some resistance has already occurred," Number Four spoke up. "I know of this stupid and clandestine operation you're planning, Dr. Methopolis. My sources are more intelligent than either you or Project Leader can imagine."

"Number Four, you have no right to infiltrate and spy on us!" Project Leader scolded.

"I am the Security Chief of Bladerdash, it's my duty to ensure this group of fifteen won't stab each other in the back like a group of psychopaths," he spoke boldly, "therefore I will monitor each and every one!" Next, the Security Chief of Balderdash poured a drink and sipped it in a swaggering manner.

"I could reach out my hand and strangle you

from where I stand for this intrusion of distrust," Dr. Methopolis said.

"Your Bluelaser powers cannot reach across the dimension of time/space continuum and the dimensional fold, so you spit mere words to me, Dr. Methopolis. We are businessmen," the Security Chief replied.

"What resistance has happened?" Number Three asked, curious.

The Security Chief answered, "Project Leader put a human man in power back in 193, Hitler, but the son-of-a-bitch wanted to kill an entire nation of people. He wanted to control the world for himself and created the Nazi Army. Hitler was a madman which Project Leader could not control."

"The Americans and a hand full of Murians interfered," Project Leader said.

"And what about Hussein? He...he...barely had an army capable of escaping from Iraq, let alone one able to take on the...the...American War Machine," the Security Chief stammered, frustrated. "I watched the whole War Soap Opera on my Dimensional TV and Hussein was a poor choice. To imagine he could whoop up discontent in an area, the Middle East? Dimensional TV viewing I admit is rather awkward," he added.

"I am dealing with the Murian issue," Dr. Methopolis put it.

"What are Murians?" Number Eight asked and then plopped a candy in his mouth.

Dr. Methopolis smiled watching Number Eight.

"Similar to Bluelaser people on Moonsteep, they possess supernatural powers given to them by the Annunaki," Dr. Methopolis explained.

"What measures have you undertaken to ensure this plan will go off without situations becoming a mess?" Number seven asked.

"Secrets remain secrets so the Security Chief will resort to old fashion spying to figure out the plans," Dr. Methopolis teased.

"Divine intervention will be needed," Project Leader said and on the monitor it showed him rubbing his hands together enjoying this moment.

Sixty seconds of silence elapsed.

Suddenly Number Eight spat out the candy. He clutched his throat choking and then began shaking in his seat before standing up. He fell to his knees and then his body melted.

"What – what happened to Number Eight?" Chief of Security demanded.

"I wanted to demonstrate, I have a very long reach, I poisoned Number Eight because he blocked my attempt to take control over planet 139413-HX," Dr. Methopolis said and snickered.

Members of Balderdash whispered amongst themselves and the number 139413 was repeated.

"Dr. Methopolis, you are…" Chief of Security paused. His fingers combed his hair, feeling a creeping sensation slithering up his spine.

"I am what?"

"You are the...Master of War," Chief of Security said.

"I appreciate that you agree with me," Dr. Methopolis said, "the surgeons of Moonsteep have infected multiple dimensions, spread out across five million worlds and it is written in the Moonsteep Medical Oath: "We are the surgeons of the ocean of space, the physical world and the space in between. Don't forget it."

Sixty more seconds elapsed.

"What do you know about this Balderdash Group?" Number Three asked.

"Economic wizards," Dr. Methopolis replied, "but the people typically seen at gatherings are figureheads, the puppet-masters are behind the scenes. Through my own private investigating skills, and befriending one of the elite who resides in a Canadian city, Britannia, I have discovered they go by the dumbass name, Puppet-Master or PM. There are a mere five thousand PMs globally out of a planet teaming at nine billion inhabitants."

"Very over populated," Chief of Security commented. "Not even on my parallel earth do we have nine billion, we inserted artificial population control after three billion," he said.

"Secret Societies seem to know how this parallel earth functions, political rivals, everyone wants their share of the pie," Project Leader said.

"This parallel earth has already achieved

space travel to its fourth world, a floating international space station, and a base on the moon," Dr. Methopolis pointed out.

"Five thousands Puppet-Masters, isn't that the basis of Moonsteep Eknakamoonknoon Economics?" Security Chief asked.

"You refer to the ancient Hockeynomics," Dr. Methopolis replied with a snap.

"How does Hockeynomics work?" Number Fourteen spoke up.

"Put simply: five players on the ice, no goalie: one centre, one right-wing, one left-wing and one left defenseman and one right defenseman. The game is played at a point-five tempo. Five is the symbol of the Emmaga, the procurators of the first Five Worlds; they came long before the Viking gods," Dr. Methopolis said.

"What do you mean, what do you mean the 'first Five Worlds'?" Chief of Security asked.

"First came the Emmaga, followed by the Annunaki, Moonsteep, Odin and his race, the Olympia people and one unknown race," Dr. Methopolis said.

"Who is this other race?"

"No one knows, but clues are scattered about the Milky Way Galaxy, and if someone does figure out who the fifth race is, they would command commerce," Dr. Methopolis said and shrugged. "I don't know who the fifth race is even with all of my power. However, the Eknakamoonknoon race on

Moonsteep is recognized as powerbrokers of multiple worlds and dimensions."

Sixty seconds of silence passed so all of this gobbledygook would sink in the minds of the members of Balderdash.

"When do you expect to make war on this parallel earth?" Chief of Security asked.

"Very soon. Details must be complete before the ambush, we will deploy the same force used on planet 0009834732-QK," Dr. Methopolis said.

"No more secrets, we will iron out a timetable for the invasion," Security Chief ordered.

Dr. Methopolis smiled agreeing. "I am departing for this parallel world to commence the first phase of the war."

"What are your plans?" Security Chief asked.

"I will be visiting my friend in Britannia, and together we shall make gruesome war against the Murians."

"Divine intervention will be needed to stop us," Project Leader said.

LEAD FOOT SYNDROME

C.J. pulled out of Queen-Knight Academy at around 4:20 pm on Sir John A. Macdonald Avenue heading south. She sat behind the wheel of a two door all-Canadian smart Stronach, with a 1616 cubic inch engine. It was painted a glossy forest green as one would see in a National Geographic Magazine. It was a hybrid. The modified engine could move up to two hundred and fifty kilometers per hour, but so long as C.J. did not push the sensitive pedal all the way to the floor, she would never earn a speeding ticket.

The interior was spacious and contained all the functions of a one million dollar vehicle, including the windshield, which had a military integrated inferred system TV screen tie-in. It allowed her to see in pitch-darkness, transforming the night into a greenish-white that enabled her to see any potential obstacles perfectly.

The surround sound speaker system allowed C.J. to listen to music, and today on the menu was superhero dramatic music played by Canada's newest and boldest band, the Super Assassins. They had such an awesome distinct sound, it was so cool, addictive like peanut butter and jam squished between two slices of thick toasted bread: delicious. The title of Track No. 3 was, Our Souls Rebuild Worlds [Electric-Cites].

"Electricity is the current surrounding our world,
Electricity streams through the air,
overseas, through mountains, into outer space, it's hurled,
We have created Electric-Cities with hands that were bare,

We are separated by an ebony screen,
Some people scream,
Electricity, particles of light,
Some people live in a darkness like night,

Some people live and have no life, incomplete,
Obsolete,
Our souls, Our souls, Our souls,
Our souls rebuild new worlds,
Our souls rebuild new worlds,
Our souls expand beyond our world,

No matter how far we extend into the sky,
We are connected by a stream of electricity,
Radio waves bounce off of satellites as they fly by,
We see others from afar on a screen of ebony,

We move faster than the speed of light,
Through the space as black as night,
But there are people who are incomplete,
Obsolete,
Our souls, Our souls, Our souls,
Our souls rebuild new worlds,
This is planet earth calling ET,
Please pick up the receiver, speak to me."

Chad sat in the passenger seat. "Thanks for the ride, Plum."

C.J. cast an expression at him. "What did you just call me?"

"Plum."

"Is that my pet name?"

"I was tinkering with the idea *Peach*, but *Plum* is better suited for a right-winger."

"I have hockey practice," C.J. said slowing down at a red light, "At five, and I am going to be late no thanks to Tammy "The Terrible". The intersection for the first red light from Queen-Knight Academy heading south was close to the Valkyrie Hotel, the family's legacy on her mother's side. It could be instantly recognized by the large flashing **V** on the roof top.

"We've been dating for a few weeks, so don't take this question out of context, but did you steal Tammy's notes on Hockeynomics?" Chad asked.

"What? What kind of idiotic question is that, Chump?" C.J. scolded.

"Boy, are you ever defensive."

"Chad, we worked at the library on our individual assignments for Mr. Beerdeer's history class, so why would I need to steal Tammy's Hockeynomics notes?"

"I need to ask, my parents are lawyers, so were my grandparents and my great grandparents, they have all worked at the Cameron-Knight Legal Firm," Chad said.

"Some boyfriend, *Chump*, my boyfriend suspects I am thief!"

"I simply asked a question: wherein did I imply you actually stole Tammy's notes?" Chad argued.

C.J. stepped on the gas as soon as the light changed green. The wheels smoked and the vehicle leaped ahead.

A pair of cherry lights lit up and a cruiser pulled out of the line of vehicles.

"C.J., slow down," Chad insisted, "you have attracted fleas."

"No thanks to you, Chump."

"Chad, not Chump, Chad," he corrected.

C.J. pulled off to the side of the road. "This is bullshit!" she thumped the steering wheel.

"Honesty in a relationship it is important," Chad said.

"Do I look like a thief? You know what I do from time to time within Ebony-Shine!"

Chad fell quiet, feeling guilty.

A knock came at the driver's window and she lowered it by electric power.

"Officer, Grant." C.J. recognized the woman officer immediately.

"C.J. Silverstar, what a pleasant way to meet. How are your parents?"

"Excellent. My Dad is no doubt solving big crimes because he is a sergeant in the RCMP, my mom is working saving lives as a Street Nurse, and my brother Ernie still dreams of becoming a Martian and going to live on the Mars colony," she replied.

"Good. Now, let me see your license and registration. You know the drill," Officer Grant said smiling.

"Bullshit," C.J. said under her breath as she pretended to sneeze.

"You're looking to catch something else if you don't take care of that cold," Officer Grant said.

When C.J. handed over the birth certificate there was a paperclip attached and Officer Grant's keen eyes spied a brown coloured $100 bill attached. She took everything with her back to the cruiser and returned ten minutes later handing back everything.

C.J. noticed right away the $100 bill was accepted.

"I won't press any charges this time, you can go. Where are you going right now, young lady?"

"To hockey practice," C.J. said, "The Queen-Knights play the Antiflick-Troopers this coming Friday."

"Well, I guess I will need to be there and watch the game. Have a nice day and go to the doctor to check on that lead foot."

"Oh yes, Officer," Chad accepted the consequences.

Officer Grant walked away.

"She took the hundred," C.J. said smiling at Chad and decided to give him a smooch. She forgot all about their argument, feeling empowered at the moment.

A new Super Assassin CD track, number titled *Win, Win, Win* played.

THE ILLUSTRATED WALL

C.J. and Chad stepped through the inner garage door connected to the large spacious foyer. He stopped and looked around him amazed and bombarded with images of folklore.

Painted on all four walls in colourful detail were images of a world long ago, including Valhalla, the Ash Yggdrasil or World-Tree, which including nine worlds and the city of Asgard. Odin was depicted in a portrait shot of his extended family along with their families.

In another illustrated image, it showed the Viking gods playing hockey against the Olympian gods, who of course scored a goal.

On another wall was an illustration of stars, including a solar system and in the background a pinwheel galaxy.

C.J. looked at Chad. "Mom is quite serious about our Valkyrie heritage."

"You are not Catholic?" Chad asked.

"My family is Valkyrie, but we accept Jesus as one of the greatest teachers, that is a no-brainer," C.J. explained. "However, my family religion is based on Odin, we fight for those that cannot help themselves, the disadvantaged and the homelessness. In the ancient world Valkyries were painted as these evil blood thirty women of savage war, but that isn't true. History is often told through oral stories and men often don't want a strong female personality."

"True," Chad agreed.

C.J. took Chad by the hand over to a portion of the illustrated history wall. "One oral story is that Thor and his wife, Brunhild, founded a new parallel world to start their own family, but it was soon invaded and in order to save their daughter they sent her to another parallel earth."

"Thor had one daughter with Brunhild. I don't know much about Viking History, I am Catholic," Chad said.

"Her name was Celestial-June, and she is the last Valkyrie," C.J. explained pointed to the various illustrations.

"You're telling me your family religion is a warrior one, is that what you're telling me?"

"Yes, Chad. And that is why I play hockey, it's a physical sport which makes my blood move and my heart race. It keeps me alive and refreshed, just like you do."

Chad at that moment turned to C.J. and they looked at one another and then they kissed.

"Valkyrie women chose their male counterparts, someone who could keep pace," she said. "My father is an RCMP sergeant, very active, brave and a former Canadian soldier who served in Afghanistan when Canada returned in 2029 to 2033."

"Hi Chad, hi C.J.."

They spun around to see a ten year old standing in the doorframe of the living room. He was chewing on a turkey and pepperoni sandwich with lettuce and tomato and a homemade spicy sauce. The sauce oozed out of the edges, but never dripped on the tiled floor.

"Ernie, are you spying on me?"

"No. I was watching…the Discovery channel… and heard the two of you speaking." Ernie chewed and talked.

"Chad, you have never officially met my genius brother, Ernie."

"Genius?" Chad asked.

"I attend Queen-Knight University, I am currently enrolled in Space Education and my major subject is physics, specializing in friction."

"Huh?" Chad asked puzzled.

"When a space ship is launched from earth… There is variable friction due to gravity pulling on the object. Friction is a form of super physics… How can a cylindrical shape reduce friction versus the pull of gravity? The bottom line in the math is all about ratios," Ernie explained.

Chad shrugged.

C.J. made a gesture of her palm going over her head.

"Ernie plans to be the family Martian."

"Colonist, C.J., I prefer the term colonist. There are three thousand humans living on the Mars colony," he said. He quickly returned to the living room putting down half the sandwich. He returned with a mug of Sodapop, a sparkling blue liquid.

C.J. and Chad put two-thumbs-up.

"Are you two finished exchanging bodily fluids?"

C.J. and Chad exchanged expressions and suddenly burst out laughing. They got the big picture immediately.

HOCKEY PRACTICE

"C.J., you are late," Coach Candice said watching the girl step onto the ice.

"Won't happen again." C.J. looked at twenty faces of teammates, especially Captain Determination.

"Second time."

"Sorry, Captain."

"Lead foot syndrome," Skylar commented, joking with teammates.

"Go around the rink, ten laps," Coach Candice instructed. "Skylar, since you are so eager to speak, join C.J., and because you are a Murian, twenty laps."

Skylar grunted.

C.J. skated around the rink warming up, no big deal.

While doing her laps, someone in the office decided to play dramatic theatrical battle music. She responded to the music skating faster, as her soul seemed to be energized.

Skylar whizzed around the rink and pulled up alongside C.J. and they exchanged smiles. They began accelerating.

The Queen-Knight teammates' attention turned away from Coach Candice, watching as the duo began circling the rink faster and faster as if they were performing laps on the Indy speedway.

The epic battle music continued to provide

accompaniment as the singers provided an operatic style of singing.

"Good God," Coach Candice said puzzled.

"Holy smokes," Sergio spoke up.

"If they don't slow down they will melt the ice," one of the teammates said.

"They are the fantastic duo, what can I say," another teammate said.

"There is no man on earth C.J. Silverstar cannot compete with as a full equal," Captain Determination said breath-taken.

Chad sat in the bleachers watching the interplay intensely. He sat on the edge of the seat wondering what on earth C.J. was trying to prove. Guys were much more muscular than girls and so it would be no surprise to see Skylar out pace C.J. and he was also a Murian who possessed supernatural powers. It didn't seem to matter, C.J. kept pace as an equal, against all common sense. How could a girl of five feet, eight inches, move with the same speed of a Murian?

Chad considered the odds of the co-ed ACHL beating an NHL team who had won the Stanley Cup. If the Queen-Knights won the Friday game versus the Antiflick-Troopers, that would pave the path to playing in Hockey-City against the Metroburb winner of the 2044 Stanley Cup. It was a bi-annual charity event played on TV that broadcasted globally to as many as three billion people. The ACHL contributed a lot to the sport of hockey on a grand scale, it was magical, but C.J. would never be accepted in the NHL. It was truly sad.

Chad understood the Thunder-Screamers played the typical rough and rambling sport within the General Ontario Division (G.O.D.). The whole league contained an estimated one thousand, players including overseas players from Europe and Russia. They were on hockey scholarships. Among the thousand players there were no girls unlike the ACHL which was co-ed. He did not understand the politics. He simply played hockey. If he had it his way he would give G.O.D. a C-minus grade for simply being staunchy.

Coaches at his level were like low-level drill sergeants because the players would need to respond, "Yes, Drill Sergeant!" and then go perform whatever order they were given out on the ice like well-oiled hockey-soldiers.

He also understood the average cost of a tripple-A player in the year 2045 was anywhere from twelve to eighteen thousand dollars as prices have soared to the cost of normal inflation. Top-of-the-line gear is a must for the best hockey athletes, but the average teenager doesn't have an executive career with a portfolio of investments to pay for it all either. Robbing a bank would only get one into trouble. Hockey is an all-out duke it out sport, and scholarships and funding from corporations are essential. He was lucky to have parents who were lawyers working for the Cameron-Knight Firm.

The music came to a came a crashing halt.

"Stop!" Coach Candice ordered irked.

C.J. and Skylar stopped, not even winded. Instead they turned and hugged other as if they were soldiers congratulating one another a job well done.

"We aren't finished, Coach," Skylar said.

"Yes, you both are. C.J., you are showing off," Coach Candice scolded.

"No I wasn't."

"Don't lie to me, young lady. Okay, let's play a scrimmage game," Coach Candice said stepping forward. "There is no sport on earth which you would not be astonishing. You are living in Canada and hockey is the religious sport of our nation and in ancient times the gods played the same sport. You know who you are."

C.J. stood silent and confused. What on earth did the Coach mean, "don't lie to me'? and, 'you know who you are?'

"You can keep up with me," Skylar said, excited, "that is awesome."

"Are you okay?" one of the teammates asked.

C.J. shrugged.

"Take your place on the ice, right-wing," Coach Candice said to C.J. with a firm attitude.

"Let's play hockey," Captain Determination encouraged.

"Right!" C.J. agreed.

Coach Candice dropped the vulcanized frozen rubber disk acting as the ref. Hockey practice began.

HOCKEYNOMICS

Friday, April 21, 2045
Morning Class
Dr. Beerdeer's History Class

C.J. stood facing fifty classmates. She wore the standard Queen-Knight school uniform, copper-red slacks and a matching long sleeve sweater. It displayed the red maple leaf in the upper left corner above the oval crest with the name Queen-Knight High School stitched inside.

"Go ahead, C.J., with your hockey history speech," Dr. Beerdeer said, making a gesture while sitting behind his desk. Upon it sat items from another time period. They were strange trinkets collected during his early years as a Canadian archeologist working in the Artic, Greenland and Siberia. He also had the typical facial features of a Murian man, a dog-face.

C.J. looked at her peers staring back at her. She smiled. She looked down at the cue cards in her twitching hands. Next, she took a breath, released it slowly, and began.

"Genesis, a single word, gave birth to the sea of imagination and spawned the dark matter ocean we call space where all the star clusters including pinwheel and irregular galaxies grow like sparkling flowers on the fable Yggdrasil Tree. There are leaves on this fable tree. The Milky Way provides all the refreshment for every one of the leaf worlds. But, I am not here to speak about the history of our universe. I would like to forward the idea from the Murian Nation Bible, that there are parallel universes.

I would like to comment about the dark matter ocean, found on our speck of a blue marble in the immenseness of the universe. Our world possesses oceans of liquid which to us appear just as immense. According to a brand new discovery, there is a second ocean beneath our world, trapped in the soil an estimated seven hundred miles down. It touches the entire world, my genius brother Ernie told me this. Life is full of oceans. Swimming through the darkness of the liquid oceans are peculiar creatures with long glittering tails.

Scientists in the field of pseudo-science claim we are trapped in the stomach of a fiery meteorite, which had exotic bacteria locked up inside and through some miracle fell into our primordial stew and thus life arose, always changing, evolving.

Approximately five hundred and fifty million years ago, life burst awake on the third planet from a G-Class star, our blue marble. Species that first appeared were slithering worms, bristle worms, glowing arthropods scurrying at unimaginable fathoms beneath the sea of imagination, making their small condominiums near hydrothermal vents. Those creatures began the Cambrian Period.

Did the Annunaki, the intelligent lizard race

from a parallel earth procreate the Murians? I don't know because I am Sumerian and I have my own Bible, I won't argue because I have good friends who are Murians and possess supernatural powers. Those Murians are excellent hockey players." C.J. deliberately paused, looking at the assorted faces in the history class, picking out Murian face teenage boys and girls and then the human faces. She shuffled the cue cards, keeping them in order.

"Evolution is our history, as a species on this blue marble evolving with a sport with J-shaped sticks, a vulcanized rubber disk, blades of steel, and our muscles propel us along an icy surface. It is a sport three thousand years old.

Hockey has evolved over the decades from just swatting a ball, to having a tool of the sport we call a puck, and it became organized into a magical sport by the NHL. The phenomenon of hockey caused players to emerge from all over the world, and on August 9th 1960, the Atlas Corporation ignited a new frontier of co-ed hockey called ACHL, the Atlas Corporation Hockey League.

The co-ed sport never got really recognized in the beginning until the 11th of September, 2002. The governments of the world recognized that co-ed hockey had erupted into a global sport, even including the Middle East and as far south as Peru and Argentina.

Six global teams were there in the beginning, the Queen-Knights; New York Butterscotch, Russian

Rhubarb, the Arab Thoroughbreds, the Valkyries, and the Antiflick-Troopers. These six teams have farm teams with the identical names. My Murian friends and I play for the Queen-Knights, and earn a part time salary. We are classified as global Triple-A for Atlas. My boyfriend, Chad, plays for the Thunder-Screamers and also earns a salary. He is also a Triple-A player, but he plays for the old fashion all-boys' team.

Hockey has evolved because through a miracle of fate and destiny the ACHL has created Hockeynomics. What can I say about Hockeynomics, an engine unlike anything this world has ever experienced, by funding homeless shelters for women and children on a global scale? One place I can think of off the top of my head, is the 21st Mission Enterprise on John McCrae Road. Hockeynomics fully supports a centre to care for the homeless people living within Britannia, a street nation of an estimated one million.

To demonstrate just how much of a powerful punch Hockeynomics has, the Atlas Corporation built the International Space Station three hundred feet above the earth. It was a three trillion dollar project. And the ISS was a stepping stone to constructing the moon base and then onto building the Mars Colony. All these accomplishments were made possible because of a sport called hockey, which encapsulates Hockeynomics.

Hockey is a sport played by the gods. Legend

tells us the Gods of Asgard played the sport, Odin was introduced to the game from a man from another world nicknamed "The Chief". Odin went in search of a new type of war, one without bloodshed, but one that would still deliver the same punch and excitement as war. He formed the Odin League after returning to Asgard. His son Thor, his adopted son, Loki, and other Agrarians found the winter sport to be heart pounding. Thor's two sons Magni and Modi played the sport. The Valkyries also played the sport according to a book I read given to me by my Aunt Brunhild, she died in battle in the Afghanistan War. The Olympian gods played hockey, and Zeus encouraged his son Apollo to play. The Atlanteans also played this sport against a team from an island-world called, Manlantean.

The Valkyrie paperback book my Aunt Brunhild gave me shed light on an ancient world before our world, and hockey was just as important sport," she said and looked down at the cue cards. She adjusted the cards and was about to continue, but saw Chad blow a kiss.

"Mr. Westwind, control your lips," Mister Beerdeer commented with a smirk.

"Without wandering off topic, on the 10th of June in 1957, John Diefenbaker went coast to coast and made speeches. He covered some thirty thousand miles, and all of this preceding his election to office. Mr. Diefenbaker spoke in major cities, Saskacity, Metroburb, Albert City, Britannia, and even spoke at the town of Queen-Knight's annual barbecue. All of his campaigning was part of his evolution to office, how he became the single most powerful Canadian Prime Minister in the twentieth century, with global influence. One would not imagine him as a person that might wield "the big stick" because he was a farm boy; he grew up on a prairie farm, but he spoke with compassion on the values of what it is to be human. The Progressive Conservative Party got voted into power in 1957. In the same year he announced in the assembly of nations that Murians residing in Canada would automatically become citizens, and would no longer require a living-passport. If there is anything about life, evolution always wins.

In Saskacity, there is the world famous Diefenbaker Complex & Education Centre that was built in 1972. Members of the Murian race, or Canada's First World race, attend to better themselves. Skylar Turnspeak, a Murian boy on the Queen-Knights team, worked with me during a summer hockey camp not far from Saskacity. He told me he would be attending the Diefenbaker Complex & Education Centre," C.J. said.

Chad responded with a slap of his palm on the school desk table. It made the pop can jump, but not off the desk. He had met Skylar on several occasions, a Murian dude who liked C.J. For whatever reason, Chad just did not like Skylar, no doubt it's because he can score goals without much effort using his supernatural powers. And so what if he got selected to play on the Queen-Knights! Chad knew he got beat by Skylar in the Ontario Regional School Olympics; he had gone out for shot-put and thought he had launched a great shot, but Skylar beat him by a full meter without really trying! *Show-Off!*

Chad had confronted Skylar full of frustration after being humiliated, he taunted Skylar to duke-it-out, but the Murian boy walked away, but not before Chad had taken a poke, "Can't you fight, moron!" Fortunately he attended the Cameron-Knight High School. He never told C.J. what he did, keeping it top secret. So what if Skylar played for the Queen-Knights.

"Mr. Westwind, settle your hormones, you are being rude," Mr. Beerdeer spoke a little louder.

C.J. cast an expression at Chad, puzzled. She continued. "Further demonstrating the power of evolution, the Canadian Government during World War two, under Prime Minister William Lyon Mackenzie King, decided to create an elite body we have come to know as H.O.C.K.E.Y. and specifically designed for Murians possessing honed supernatural powers and employed as H.O.C.K.E.Y. Players. We don't call our people "agents" as the CIA does. The H.O.C.K.E.Y. Players protect us Canadian similar to CSIS and the RCMP and again, evolution always wins. It is an acronym of course, but I won't bother to go into boring detail as many of you are aware of its meaning," she said and once again adjusted the cue cards to the last two.

Fazillah gave a pair of thumbs-up.

Simultaneously a blonde girl spat out a small paper ball through a plastic straw. The small ball smacked the back of Chad's neck. He shifted while sitting in the desk and the legs of the desk scraped the floor.

"Mr. Westwind, is there something wrong?" Mr. Beerdeer asked curiously.

"Uhhh…Nothing…" Chad stumbled pretending to be innocent. His hand knocked an open pop can off the desk.

"Busted," Tammy whispered a scolding comment.

Chad's head turned to the blonde girl just to the left and two seats further back in the third row.

Chrissy stood up at nearly light speed and outstretched her right arm. She exerted mental supernatural energy releasing a humming sound. The pop can stopped mid-way through the fall and turned up right. The liquid contents remained inside. She swished her hand and the pop can went right into the garbage can at the front of the class.

Mr. Beerdeer stood up displaying an angry expression. "Chrissy, you are showing off. It was merely Chad's pop can. We will speak later and I don't care if your father is a Russian industrial tycoon, so don't bother to suspect you can threaten me. I too possess supernatural powers as you can see from my face. C.J., please continue. And no more comments until after C.J. is finished, is that clear?

Otherwise, I will fail anyone else that speaks out."

Sixty seconds of silence came.

"I began my History Speech using the word "genesis": hockey has evolved as you now watch the NHL and ACHL on TV. It supports major global projects through Hockeynomics. The ancient world played the sport. In closing I simply want to say the Homo-Sapien species has risen above its origins, has achieved a bold new frontier by colonizing Mars through a mere sport with the engine of Hockeynomics. It remains a mystery how the gods figured it all out. Who did Odin meet? Who is the mysterious "Chief"? How does a mere sport reach into depth of our souls, pushing our emotions to such a state of frenzy and lift us into outer space? I guess the origins of hockey will remain as much as enigma as who really built the pyramids upon the Giza Plateau. Are we being prepared for a new type of battle, and how does hockey fit into this picture? Thank you."

Chad burst to his feet applauding before anyone else.

Mr. Beerdeer smiled. For the first time the boy got it right!

H.O.C.K.E.Y.

Meanwhile, hundreds of kilometers away, in the Russell-Prescott County of Ottawa Region, a digital clock's third digit flicked. It was now 7:53 am at the H.O.C.K.E.Y. headquarters.

BOOM!

Sheet lightning pulsated and the moleskin cloud transformed becoming a purple glow.

On the outskirts of Ottawa sat a building with sloping sides that dripped continuously. The torrent of rain pelleted the tinted windows. The structure resembled the legendary Maple Leaf Gardens in Toronto, now the Hockey Hall of fame. A nine foot fence topped with razor sharp spiral barbwire wrapped its way around H.O.C.K.E.Y. headquarters, covering an estimated five kilometers. The lawn contained several indigenous Canadian short Murian trees. The mowed grass blew in waves, stirred by the gusts of wind.

The single narrow road leading to H.O.C.K.E.Y. H.Q. was precisely three kilometers long, and CCTVs spied every vehicle camouflaged in the trees. The forest became like a funnel around the road. A security booth at the entrance had five heavily armed RCMP officers posted twenty-four hours a day, seven days a week, checking all employee credentials.

"Is this dog supposed to be with you, Coach

Savage?" the young looking RCMP officer asked.

"New?"

"Yes, Sir."

"Meet Star-Dog, his rank and file are on record with a retinal scan," the coach replied and pointed to the military dog tag that read:000987654321, and which included a barcode.

"This dog has a rank?"

"He is listed on active duty as General Star-Dog, originally born on planet Rawhide Bone within the Constellation Dog House approximately twelve light years from earth's Butterfly Constellation," the Coach explained in a casual tone and provoked a smile from the young RCMP officer.

"I fully understand, Sir."

"You haven't got a clue if I am telling you the truth or spinning a fantasy story," the Coach said, "Go back to your business, Constable."

The officers turned their attention back to the NHL hockey game on the laptop, the Saskacity Indians versus the Metroburb Snow Geese. The Snow Geese were ahead five to three.

H.O.C.K.E.Y. coach Terry Savage parked the all-blue government car inside an underground garage. The car resembled a standard two-door Stronach Thunder-Runner equipped with classified security features. At the rear portion there was a velocity attachment to ensure it would keep ground when travelling at top speed. The top speed however was classified. Upon command it would perform like a race car. Painted on the engine hood was something Coach Savage had deliberately ordered on all the H.O.C.K.E.Y. vehicles: a pair of hockey sticks crossed over to form an X.

The driver's door slid all the way back electronically.

He got out accompanied by an unleashed four legged furry friend, a Jack-Russell Terrier mix. Savage spoke, "General Star-Dog, do you have to make water?" The companion gave a bark. And so the two pals ventured outside through a side garage door so Star-Dog could make water on his other favourite friend, a bright red fire hydrant.

Coach Savage held an umbrella.

BOOM!

Star-Dog returned waging his short tail. The dog-tag on the black collar indicated he was Canadian property. Coach Savage had included a doggie bowtie, presenting him as a gentleman dog, not some run-of-the-mill mutt.

"Good boy." Coach Savage rubbed behind his ears gently and got a bark in return. "Right you are, it's pouring."

The two pals went to the front glass doors. Coach Savage pressed a security card against a black "reader" which allowed the red-eye to scan the barcode. The doors separated allowing the pals to get inside.

A pair of armed security officers at the front desk watched the hockey game, but the Asian man gave a nod acknowledging Coach Savage.

The pals walked over to the elevator and rode up to a mid-level section above the security zone. They soon stepped inside what seemed to be an elevator. Once inside, he inserted a black key inside a slot and twisted it all the way right and the rear of the elevator opened and the pals stepped inside a secret elevator.

The secret elevator took them to a secret floor sandwiched between to regular floors.

Stepping out of the elevator, they entered the secret floor. The first image on the polished tiles was a large crest with dozens of red and white Maple Leafs on the outer circle, the inner circle containing a picture of a Canadian beaver. Coach Savage actually ordered the emblem to be a wet land creature such as a beaver because it represented stability in the water and the beaver was a symbol of ingenuity because it could build damns for a home. The creature implied the Canadian Navy should always be as clever as a beaver and for the combat soldier on land the beaver represented the ability to camouflage his home in plain sight with whatever was available. Also, the sharp front teeth represent a natural weapon and a soldier should always be prepared with a hunting knife as a weapon for self-defence or to kill a rodent like a rabbit for food, but worms are also good to eat and loaded with protein.

A semi-circular desk faced the elevator where three people sat doing multi-tasking jobs. A large mural behind the semi-circle depicted Canadian hockey heroes of the twentieth century i.e. Tim Horton, Bobby Orr, Gretzky, Angela James, Theadora Imbrogno and Abby Hoffman.

"Good morning, Coach Savage," the Murian woman behind the desk said and smiled. The cat face whiskers twitched.

"And the same, Ms. Turtle-Cat."

"Check the Can-Globetrotting News Network ASAP," Ms. Turtle-Cat suggested and wiggled her square-cat eyebrows.

"Thanks for the tip."

General Star-Dog gave three barks and in response, several heads popped out of several offices along the hall.

"Good morning, General," several staff members said.

A Murian man approached General Star-Dog and gave a deliberate salute.

"Winter-Giant at your service, Sir!" And he continued about his business, but not without exchanging a high-five with Coach Savage.

The two comrades stepped inside an office at the end of the hall. Coach Savage removed the trench coat and hung it up in a closet. Next, he began brewing a single cup of coffee and while that brewed he gave his partner a doggie treat.

General Star-Dog went over to his bed and curled up with a milk bone. He would save it for a snack for later.

Soon Coach Savage sat at his desk facing a ready-to-go laptop. He put the coffee down on a cork coaster. He pressed "the Quick-On" button. The black screen dissolved presenting a crest with the word H.O.C.K.E.Y. The clock in the lower right hand corner read 8:37 AM. He clicked the arrow-curser on "News" at the top of the screen.

" – For those of you just tuning in, we just arrived twenty-five minutes ago, and we are live. This is the Can-Globetrotting News Network, CGNN, I am Globetrotting reporter Betty Pagliaro, inside the Canadian Artic Triangle on Atlas Island." She tried to squeeze in as much verbal information as possible.

Coach Savage sat watching the HDTV broadcast on the laptop, rubbing his chin with concern. He dipped a cookie into the creamy coffee and took a bite.

Crunch!

"The Canadian Navy, as you can see behind me, is very active with three dozen men doing something. I am unsure as to exactly what they are doing, But they are off the coast of Atlas Island – Get a shot of the coast," Reporter Pagliaro said to the cameraman.

Coach Savage could see the camera jiggling as the cameraman attempted to steady it and focus on the aircraft carrier.

Crunch!

"The Queen Annadada is Canada's first

aircraft carrier designed specifically for the Artic. Built in 2042, at a cost of one billion dollars, created more taxes for the poor guy to shell out. Navy Commander Copper Silverstar is in charge. His older brother is the Canadian Admiral Greg Silverstar. If our viewers are unaware, the Silverstar family originates from Scotland and is an industrial military family," Reporter Pagliaro explained quickly.

The cameraman moved the camera around, attempting to record as much visual detail as possible, but Canadian Navy men stood blocking the cameraman's movements.

"Stay behind the taped off area, Sir," one man ordered. He was clad in Artic Navy gear.

"If you refuse to cooperate we will force you to swim," a second man spoke up.

"Commander Silverstar gave us permission, this is our report by invitation, and we were already aboard the Queen-Annadada. We were invited by the Canadian Navy brass to do a report on the first floating Artic Aircraft," Reporter Pagliaro argued as she confronted the Navy men. Next, she began marching closer to the group of senior Navy Officers and the cameraman followed.

"Switchboard," Coach Savage said picking up the puck shaped intercom. He was merely required to speak into it.

"Turtle-Cat listening."

"Uplink H.O.C.K.E.Y. to Artic Triangle and let me speak with Commander Silverstar."

"Right away," Turtle-Cat replied. The laptop's clock now read 9:01 AM.

Crunch!

Bases across Canada began reporting in; the Artic Base a.k.a. Snow Base, the Newfoundland Base a.k.a. Lobster, the Quebec Base a.k.a. Champlain, the prairie base a.k.a. Buffalo, Vancouver Station a.k.a. HMCS Sioux. Coach Savage knew a little military history of the HMCS Sioux; it had patrolled the waters of the Yellow Sea during the Korean War in the 1950s.

If Canadians knew the real reason why an estimated thirty thousand Canadian soldiers had gone into hyperactive action fighting in Korea, it would start a revelation of the strangest degree. The Korean War was the first United Nation's War to prevent the hostile group, the Balderdash Group, from supplying the Koreans with nuclear power!

Coach Savage remembered his grandfather telling him that his great, great grandfather got involved in the Korean War conflict and met two brothers from the Silverstar clan from Scotland. The Silverstar military-industrial family provided state-of-the-art equipment to help battle robots which were designed to protect a nearly finished nuclear facility.

God only knows where the robots originated.

On the first Tuesday in July 1955, at 4:03 in the morning, D-Day was declared for Balderdash. A fifty-man troop of Canadians accompanied by a mere ten supernatural Murians smashed the secret base.

The unfinished nuclear facility was demolished, where they had found four rocket bays, which had contained dirty bombs.

Communication crackled over the H.O.C.K.E.Y. phone. "This is Navy Commander Silverstar, what's up, Coach? I am unsure why I am getting static on the line, can you hear me alright?"

"Just fine, Commander. I can see you on my laptop screen. Clear that reporter away!"

"That's why we've been friends so long, I like your spunk. You order the entire world around like you own it. Regardless, I can do that, Sir." He replied with a mock salute.

"I am sending Winter-Byrd and Winter-Giant to Atlas Island for a closer observation."

"I haven't got any issues with that. You won't believe what fell out of the sky!"

"There is a lot of junk floating in orbit," Coach Savage commented wryly, but keep in good spirit.

"How about a hammer from a parallel dimensional universe?" Commander Silverstar said teasing.

"Can you lift it?" Coach Savage asked and smirked.

"Yeah." Commander Silverstar picked up the hammer showing how easy it was to pick it up. "It's like a feather, no weight whatsoever."

"It certainly doesn't belong to Thor, because nobody can lift Thor's hammer."

"It has the image of a stone face and strange writing engraved on the blue rock it is made from," Commander Silverstar said.

"I am sending two H.O.C.K.E.Y. Players to bring the hammer back to the Stadium for closer inspection. My players will be in the Artic shortly," Coach Savage said.

A few minutes later, Winter-Byrd and Winter-Giant stepped inside the office and seated themselves facing their boss.

"A new gig?" Winter-Byrd asked.

Coach Savage handed them a piece of paper with a latitude and longitude location. "Bring back the prize ASAP."

"Sounds cool," Winter-Giant replied. He continued speaking in the usual Murian idiom-filled lingo. "It looks to be pretty much a black and white job."

"Winter-Giant, we had better hit the road," Winter-Byrd agreed.

"Speak English," Coach Savage teased. "It's not clear if this alien hammer is a gift, eh, so retrieve it so we can find out what it is. Play with a hockey stick, not a hammer."

"Playing with an alien hammer could be like striking a matchstick," Winter-Byrd replied.

The friends shared a knowing look.

"Just remember, you are H.O.C.K.E.Y. Players, not GI. Joes, and you work in the great white north!" Coach Savage joked again. "Let this assignment be the first period."

Winter-Byrd and Winter-Giant stepped outside into the unusually warm rain, and using their Murian supernatural powers of aerokenisis, lifted skyward. At two thousand feet, they stopped and then flew at bullet-speed toward their destination. The uniforms they wore were identical, a red and white uniform with a maple leaf in the centre of their chests.

**

Then, at 9:35 a.m.:

Boom!

Coach Savage paused his typing on the laptop in mid-sentence at the eruption of thunder. He spun around, curious. Rising to his feet, he approached the tinted window which could not be seen on the exterior of the building. It was camouflaged within the artistic paint job.

On the illustrated wall on that particular portion of H.O.C.K.E.Y. headquarters, was a large mural of more assorted early twenty-first century hockey players. The faces of Mario Yzerman, who played from 1985 –2002, Erik Roloson (2002 – 2020), and two of the women; Valerie Francis (2019 – 2030), and May Frostberg (2020 to 2040) gleamed down at all who passed by.

The window the coach peered through had been designed to appear as the pupil of a hockey player, unknown in modern times because the player had originated from the land of Sumeria, an estimate eight thousand years ago. Coach Savage knew the ancient player as Captain Rhubarb Parflickle.

He spied through the pupil-window the three dozen satellite array systems, which scanned ten million forms of communication under the unique defense program P.U.C.K. The satellites of the Paranormal Unlimited Canadian Kaleidoscope, could hone-in on exotic energy released by areas of the earth that were classified as very dangerous. The Bermuda Triangle, Devil's Triangle, the Artic Triangle and the Antarctica Triangle were constantly watched among any other areas that drew the system's curious eye. It could also hone-in on supernatural people, the Murians, for example.

A three prong of lightning flashed.

A musical beep came on the H.O.C.K.E.Y. phone: *beep, da-da-beep-beep!* Savage nicknamed it the eavesdrop phone. He picked up the cell phone.

"Ms. Turtle-Cat Is this line secure?" he asked.

"Yes. It's General Thunder-Bay."

A click occurred, uplinking the phones.

"Coach Savage, can you hear me?"

"Is there a new H.O.C.K.E.Y. game, General Thunder-Bay?"

"Dream-Snatcher and Metalloid have escaped from the Saskacity penalty box."

"How?" Savage demanded, projecting his voice louder than normal in shock.

"You had better wake up two defensemen,"

the General ordered keeping the conversation short.

"You are evading my question."

"I haven't got all the answers, I'm just a general."

"Good excuse," Savage said rolling along, "And I have two perfect young Murian H.O.C.K.E.Y. players in mind; Zam Smart, code name Metaflesh, and his partner Ms. Ordinary a.k.a. the Murian Madusa, not to be confused with Medusa," Savage said adding the tidbit of information.

"Thank you for the English lesson," General Thunder-Bay said wryly. "I was thinking of Iron-Will and Plasma," he commented.

"Iron-Will and Plasma are over three hundred years old, retirement age for Murians. And besides, they served Canada during the First World War, Second World War, the Korean War, the Cold War, and saved JFK from Warrior's assassination attempt."

"I know Warrior has been rotting away inside the Saskacity Supermax Prison, don't remind me, because he attempted a breakout sixteen months ago," General Thunder-Bay said.

The Bullet that Changed Camelot, the 1960s headlines had read. Some Hollywood big shot had even directed a movie by the same name.

General Thunder-Bay chewed on a cigar, listening to Coach Savage, while sitting in his office in a secret location. "Enough chit-chat, go with your recommendations. You better be on the money, you don't need a midlife crisis, and you are the youngest head of H.O.C.K.E.Y. Savage, so don't embarrass your ego."

"I first met Zam and Madusa during my first tour in the Second Afghan Conflict 2024 to 2028. I can personally speak for them from our shared history in battle. We resided at the Kandahar Base. I just sent you an email so read it, it's about my two defensemen. All of it is top secret, but it would make a good movie." The men shared a laugh understanding tight-lipped issues.

"I am glad you returned to Canadian soil in one piece," General Thunder-Bay said.

"Sir, my right arm is bionic as a result of an incident during that Afghanistan conflict."

Uncomfortable seconds of silence passed between the men.

"I returned to Canada, and eventually became the Coach of H.O.C.K.E.Y.," Coach Savage said.

"The Murian people selected you, Savage, because you risked your life well above the call of duty saving one of their own and I will let you in on a wee secret: top Murians of H.O.C.K.E.Y. were filing their notice of resignation just to place you at the top of the food chain."

"I had no idea, I thought it was fate or destiny." He popped a handful of salted peanuts into his mouth.

"Go with your Murian H.O.C.K.E.Y. players, Zam and Madusa," General Thunder-Bay agreed. "Where do they live?"

"They're in the famous Murian Enclave inside Queen-Knight. Three thousand Murians live there, in a rural area with farms. It's quite attractive, almost like a tourist attraction. I will alert communications to wake up our H.O.C.K.E.Y. players," Savage said.

"Keep me posted." The General disconnected their call.

Savage kept his cellphone open. "Communication department, uplink my phone to H.O.C.K.E.Y. players Metaflesh and Madusa," he ordered.

"Understood, Sir! You are now uplinked," the male voice said.

DUKE CAMERON KNIGHT

The Town of Queen-Knight has a population of one million, three hundred thousand five, seven hundred and nine. It is the capital of Canada, and has been since 1867 when it was incorporated by Buckingham Palace. Duke Cameron Knight founded it way back in 1812, two hundred and thirty-three years ago.

That blurb can be found on any entry points connecting Queen-Knight to the rest of Ontario. It is one hundred and fifty-five kilometers east of Britannia, a powerful twenty-first century city. York, also known as Toronto, was smack-dab between them. It is the only town in all of Canada for which the main strip is named after Canada's first Prime Minister, Sir John A. Macdonald. The motto for the town is Latin: *spiritus locus*, but translated into English means, "The spirit of the place". The duke had always thought of it as having a guardian deity.

The Queen-Knight sports and recreation centre was located on Diefenbaker Street. The Knight family had owned the land since 1812, since the English duke had founded it. Hockey was and had always been, a predominant sport there. Over the years it had undergone various re-constructions and changes, and now in 2045, it once again had a state-of-the-art recreation building with various indoor sports. It boasted three hockey rinks.

The Cameron Knight family also named the famous street Diefenbaker, after a staunch supporter for the underdogs. They have law offices in Queen-Knight and Metroburb City, located seventy-five kilometers to the south. Rapid transportation helped shuffle everyone about.

The gleaming Cameron Knight Skyscraper was in the core of Metroburb along with several other skyscrapers including the Tereshkova skyscraper. The Cameron Knight legal firm helped support the underdogs on a global scale, fighting corruptions in the same league as the Atlas Corporation. On several occasions the Atlas Corporation has assisted by sharing cases they deemed worthy, for the Cameron Knight firm could economically handle them.

"Mr. and Ms. Westwind," the receptionist addressed the lawyers, stepping inside the office, "The Murian family is here."

"Show them inside," Mr. Westwind encouraged.

A mother and father entered the office dressed in typical Murian fashion. The fabric was made of a supernatural material that kept it from eroding like regular cloth so it could last a person's lifetime. It was not indestructible. Winter-Byrd and Winter-Giant like other H.O.C.K.E.Y. players, wore the fabric as part of their Canadian uniform. It saved the government a few loonies and toonies from buying more uniforms.

"The weather is not fine, so don't ask," the

father barked, annoyed, and began pacing immediately. Objects in the room began rattling.

"Settle your supernatural powers, please, Dear!" the wife scolded, "These lawyers were recommended to us by Iron-Will and Plasma," the wife said standing nervously.

"Please sit and start at the beginning," Ms. Westwind encouraged, making a gesture to the couple.

"I-I don't know where to start. Our child is sick. He is losing his…abilities. I-I don't know how to speak on this matter. I teach our son to behave and here I-I am, in a legal firm!" The Murian man stammered in frustration.

Long seconds of silence went by.

"What are your names?" Mr. Westwind asked in a calm voice.

"I am Shepard and this is my wife, Be-Good. We are simple Murian farmers from the Queen-Knight Enclave," he said and sitting down.

"You just said your son is ill?" Ms. Westwind asked.

"Can you describe the nature of the symptoms?" Mr. Westwind followed.

"How is it you are so sure your son is losing his supernatural powers?" Ms. Westwind added.

Shepard clapped his palms together so hard that the room rattled and items fell about. "One question at a time," he insisted.

Be-Good spoke up, "Symptoms include a

swelling headache, five to eight small chicken pock-like bulbs on the left temple, pale eyes as opposed to our naturally opaque pupil, and mutating into a sickly colour. In other medical exams dark brown smudges were also found."

"We know the direct cause of this sickness," Shepard said.

"You do?" The husband and wife lawyer exchanged expressions.

"Don't laugh at us."

"No, we won't," Ms. Westwind said.

Shepard pulled out of a cloth bag a can of Sodapop. "Our son has adopted a strange liking to this sweet product, Sodapop, produced and manufactured by Zip-Cool industries, the world's supplier of several soft drinks. It is owned by a Dr. Methopolis," he said.

Mr. Westwind reached out and took the can in hand. It was unopened.

"Our son, Chad, drinks Sodapop, but he has never gotten sick," Ms. Westwind commented puzzled.

"I want this – *we* want this product investigated," Be-Good ordered. From her pocket, she produced ten sheets of folded paper and proceeded to open them. "I have gone to various parents asking for signatures to back up our inquiry for an investigation by the RCMP."

The husband and wife lawyer team once again exchanged expressions without saying a word for a minute.

"How is your son?"

Shepard took a deep breath of air and let out the answer. "He died last month."

The team of lawyers felt as though they had been suddenly struck by an invisible hammer, perhaps one with the same power Thor wielded when commanding thunderstorms.

"We will look into this immediately, Shepard and Be-Good," Ms. Westwind assured them, rising to her feet like a titan and followed by her husband. They shook hands.

"At Cameron Knight, you only pay when we win," Mr. Westwind said.

"Our son, he was our only child. Be-Good cannot bare another child, her womb won't accept a second, but we adopted two Murians," Shepard explained.

"Your case is in good hands at the Cameron Knight Legal Firm," Ms. Westwind said.

STREET NURSE
(A Personal Note from Kate Silverstar)

Drugs can be derived from plants, ephedrine, ipecacuanha, quinine and some originate from microorganisms like penicillin, streptomycin and vaccines. Another type of drugs can be found in animal sources i.e. heparin, insulin and antitoxins. At the end of the day, they are transformed into serums by scientists and the anatomy reacts to injections either positively or negatively.

I was stationed in Britannia fifteen years ago in 2030, two years after my husband, Gary Silverstar, a former lieutenant in the Canadian military, returned home for good. He served two tours in Kandahar upon Canada returning for another mission in 2024 to 2028 to once again give freedom to women and children so they may get an education without being subjects of tyranny or abuse or brainwashing. At the time Gary was just eighteen, but he returned home promoted to lieutenant for distinguished service and bravery above the call of duty and enrolled into the RCMP. Call it fate.

We were destined to be married as we had attended Queen-Knight Academy just like my daughter C.J. and her boyfriend Chad would later do. Gary had been crowned the most likely to succeed at graduation while, yeah, I was the prom queen and he was prom king. Once again, call it providence.

Our lives it seemed, would be spent fighting the drug wars. While stationed in Kandahar, Gary and his faithful dog, Corporal Jupiter, a giant suck-up German Shepard, single-handily broke up a powerful drug empire run by a mysterious man named General Wrinkle. Gary managed to infiltrate the organization by going undercover alone. He informed one of his friends of his intentions and to get word back to his superiors at the Kandahar base. He worked his way to the inner circle over a nine week period, and as for Corporal Jupiter, he would tell drug insiders: "This is my dog, he is my bodyguard." The joked seemed to work because other men got along well with the German-Shepard suck-up!

When the shipment, ten tons of heroin, got loaded inside a ship bound for Canada, it was destined for the streets of Britannia, Metroburb, Saskacity and Albert-City at a street value of several million dollars. As it got closer to the St. Lawrence Seaway, Gary went into hyper-action taking control of the communication room and sending out a pre-arranged code single to the Canadian military coastguard.

At the tender age of eighteen Gary Silverstar had busted up a major drug shipment bound for Canadian cities. And with his military skill, he in fact used an assault gun to take down several members of a group called, the Henchmen. He was excellent at hand-to-hand combat, demonstrating to the punks on the boat that Canadian soldiers are the best trained.

But why should that surprise me, my husband comes from a bloodline of soldiers, a military family originating in Scotland, like Canada's first prime minister, Sir John A. Macdonald, combat was already bred into his DNA. He learned to fight as a child, taking lessons in mixed martial arts as our daughter C.J., is now.

The vessel was surrounded and boarded and the sailors aboard were captured. The drugs were seized by the RCMP, with assistance from elite H.O.C.K.E.Y. players. The supernatural officers Metaflesh, Winter-Giant, Winter-Byrd and Madusa captured the bad ass Murians, Metalloid and Dream-Snatcher.

Gary told me the entire story during bedtime one night, and it let me sleep securely to know that my husband was capable of stopping the creeps in this world.

Gary spent time at home with me and returned to Kandahar for a second tour, but this time was placed in a group of drug hunters. He left when I became pregnant with C.J. He watched me give birth via the internet while at the Kandahar Base. I don't believe we have ever been closer while so far away simultaneously.

Gary took over as group leader when his commander got seriously wounded in a fire fight while taking on rebel soldiers. His commander died at the Kandahar base and upon returning to Canada, travelled the Highway of Heroes.

Gary got out of military action and entered into the RCMP's drug enforcement integrated unit. It was a no-brainer, the type of career he would receive commendations for after demonstrating an uncanny ability to find drugs. Corporal Jupiter became a part of our family, a kissy-kissy friend to C.J., and later to our son Ernie.

I am glad Gary is at home because he was with me when our son was born. Ernie G. Silverstar, the family's soon-to-be Canadian astronaut living on the Mars colony and currently attending Queen-Knight University at the impressive age of twelve. I am blessed with two super smart kids, so I do say thank you to Odin, the Alfather of my Viking background.

Working in Britannia with the homeless, the drugs on the streets are an issue. You name it, it can be bought, blue pills, pink pills, red ones, alcohol, amphetamines, etc. Go-Go Juice is a common one: caffeine loaded drinks mixed with pink pills and that will certainly place the pulmonary rate on an accelerator that has no speed limit. When a patient crashes, I am told it feels like being slammed into the ground head first from the cockpit of a supersonic jet.

Medical School doesn't prepare nurses for the intense street action: there are no programs that give students real-world scenarios to combat the war zone I am confronted with each day in Britannia, Canada's mecca of business and trade. It is pretty much left to run itself. One could easily become disillusioned if one doesn't have a clear sense of duty and why they are working in Britannia. However, the homeless people call the city of glass and dark towers by another name, Ebony-Shine.

Former Prime Minister Diefenbaker "the Chief", visited Britannia while crossing Canada to get elected into office. He toured the streets flanked by a staff of supporters. The speech he gave in the 1958 resonates in history classes across Canada.

This is paraphrasing the former "Chief", and what he had to say about Britannia in 1958, "I see a city of towers and weaving between them are dingy alleyways where people coexist in a shanty inner-city, so do not believe for one second poverty is gone, it lingers in every nook and cranny. While our American neighbors have Hollywood, merely sparkling jewelry which can be traded for cash or for a sport coup, I believe that people are not a commodity and should never be traded for cash or a set of golf clubs. As Prime Minister, I will aim to bring Thor's hammer upon Britannia and break up the icy grip it holds on the shanty inner-city. No longer will fat cats sit it their lofty plush offices, I am placing Britannia on notice!"

While in office, "the Chief" indeed wielded a thrust of power to help the impoverished, waging a non-stop war against Britannia which seemed to withstand every type of policy he mustered. It seemed to possess a supernatural Berlin Wall that showed no sign of cracking under pressure.

In and around the same time "the Chief" conducted his attacks against Britannia, the mysterious Street Surgeon made appearances on the streets. The Homeless people claim she performed various miracle methods of surgeries including delivering babies. If the Street Surgeon does exist, I have never encountered this person and the pictures in the newspapers are blurry at best.

I am employed though the Atlas Corporation Care Division, reporting each time to Enterprise Mission 21 located on John McCrea Avenue, named after the author of the poem "In Flanders Fields", from the First World War. Working currently within Britannia are a hard-core group of five hundred Street Nurses, our medical tools tucked inside utility belts we wear as part of our uniform, which includes a cape and a hood. We work rain or shine because homelessness doesn't take a day off when it's soggy outside or on cold winter nights.

Current victims living on the streets of Britannia suffer from a roster of issues other than drugs, which include head injuries for various reasons, headaches, hemorrhoids, various rashes, urinary issues, but diabetes is the major concern as it has become on a global basis according to W.H.O. alerts. There are people that experience bowel obstruction, ear infections and mental health issues.

I carry with me at all times slung over my shoulder a black medical bag, and inside various pockets are medical drugs supplied by the Atlas

Pharmaceutical Division. The Atlas Corporation owns more patents than any other corporation on earth.

My family bloodline of Vikings has been involved with the Atlas Care Division for generations. It appears C.J. won't be, as she would rather be a hockey player in the ACHL. With what I face each day, I am glad she had found a new possible career, perhaps starting a new bloodline career for the generations that follow.

My up-line is Street Surgeon Scarlette Reece, a medical soldier enlisted in the Atlas Corporation. She is the commander of Enterprise Mission 21, which puts her in charge of twenty-five base staff, and five hundred Street Nurses. Working on the street is done in a co-ed format, and people from an assortment of nations Have joined. A number of us are able to speak as many as five languages, and several people can speak a staggering ten. I speak three: English, French and German. Street Surgeon Reece can speak a multitude of languages fluently.

The ten story building is equipped with three emergency rooms complete with treatment table, X-ray machine, overhead spotlight, I.V. poles, a monitor for EKG, a defibrillator, a container for the disposal of biohazard waste, suction machines and gurney carts. The types of tools of the trade that are within the Atlas Corporation's medical umbrella, are somewhat different than in regular hospitals. All of the staff become trained in how to use the fantastic equipment.

One day, I looked downward from the sky while flying inside my daughter's Silver-Bird. All of the tiny narrow alleyways twisting between offices, businesses and houses that I walk through on my beat, are camouflaged by buildings. It is truly an inner-city. The main streets are visible and no one would require binoculars to see them, but binoculars would be useful to locate a few pathways. It gave off the impression of wealth and power.

The most visible object was the quick mass transit system, the figure eight monorail track circling Britannia. A high speed bullet train sped through the city limits.

Britannia is supposed to be the most powerful symbol of commerce in Canada, yet trapped within are nearly one million souls in search of hope. It has become a human war to save lives.

In the heart of Britannia are five super skyscrapers that belong to the Canoe family of businesses. They are interconnected by transparent walkways. They form a horse-shoe which is supposed to bring good fortune.

How long will the Canoe family continue to possess such a powerhouse monopoly, and when will our government wake up to see the homeless souls?

I thought back to the time I found myself sitting next to C.J. in the family SUV and on the radio came Canada's newest rock sensation, Super Assassins. I recall the lyrics of the song sung by one time student of Queen-Knight Academy, Roy

Mackenzie:

"These transparent windows of fake gold bars
Plugged into the soil where men and women toil,
These transparent windows of fake gold bars
Sixty plus stories tall, but the forgotten souls will fall
Bones of my bones
Bones of my bones
Bones of my bones built with sweat of the brow
Bones of my bones built with sweat of the brow
And all I ask for bread in return is a place to call
home where I may sojourn."

As I recall, the Super Assassins donated all money from that song to raising food for the homeless in Britannia.

THIRD PERIOD

Booming over the stadium speakers played a song by 1990s rock group, Megadeath, "Blood of Heroes". That song was ancient considering this was 2045, but it still packed a punch.

Athletes glided on blades of razor sharp steel while stick handling an inch thick vulcanized frozen rubber disk, deeking out opponents and hoping not to be slammed against the boards. It often happens without warning and a teeth rattling *Bam!*

C.J.'s jersey baring the number 444 spun about three times with the impact, and she went down, but she managed to keep her grasp on the wooden stick. Throughout her inner anatomy, her ribcage which protected all of the vital organs, heart, liver, pancreas, kidneys and lungs, she felt a coursing pain surging through her bones, but she refused to allow the pins-and-needles to affect her; no pain no gain. Fortunately the padding of the uniform protected her, but her hand felt around briefly to make sure she was really alright. It is an instinct to be sure, to confirm vital areas are not smashed. She felt extremely okay. She wanted to get back into action. *Whew!*

The song clip ended.

Despite the rough-and-tumble play, none of the dudes in black and white striped jerseys called for a penalty.

Parents and fans in the stands booed the Refs.

Skylar stopped skating approached C.J., kneeling beside her on the frozen battlefield.

C.J. spied the Hindu ref as he exchanged a curious expression, but she gave him a gesture everything was okay. He responded with a frown, unsure what she was implying, either telling him off or being friendly. He positioned the whistle at his lips ready to blow, but then backed off not wishing to stop the play.

Displayed on the digital scoreboard was the score 4-5. C.J. had no intention of lagging behind the visiting team. The Antiflick-Troopers originated from the town of the same name, Antiflick, located on the outskirts of Saskacity. Saskacity was close to Prince Albert National Park. This was the last game for 2045, the team that won this one would go to Hockey-City and play the NHL team that won the Stanley Cup from the previous season.

C.J. nodded to Skylar and stood up under her own powers to demonstrate to her teammate she could finish this battle.

In the bleachers, C.J.'s family stood up cheering her on.

"Astonishing," Ernie said turning to look at his mom. He snacked on a carrot *crunch!* His mother did not want him eating too much junk food. Before every bite he would dip the end into a dressing. *Crunch!*

"I cannot believe C.J. was able to regain her

breath," Nurse Silverstar said sitting in the traditional Street Nursing uniform. At her feet was the all black medical bag.

"C.J. is rough n' ready," Sgt. Silverstar replied sipping a drink.

"I wonder where Chad is," Ernie said.

In net for the Queen-Knights, was Luna Juno a.k.a. Tiger-Girl, who ranked in *Sea of Immagination Magazine's* "Youth Hockey" section in the top ten goalies. As a player in the co-ed version of a traditionally all-male dominated sport, the sports writer compared Tiger-Girl to Russian player Vladislav Tretiak, who played on the ancient Red Machine during the Summit Series of 1972, seventy-three years ago.

She performed the splits, blocking yet another shot from Antiflick-Troopers' number 223. The game puck bounced off the goalie padding and went wild. Tiger-Girl scrambled forward attempting to scoop it up. She punched the air with a goalie glove frustrated how fast the game toy could ricochet away. She scrambled back into position.

Parents and hockey fans cheered, responding to the action.

"I think C.J. is hurt," Ernie suspected turning to his father, who for some reason had decided to wear the entire bright red uniform of the Mounties to tonight's game. "Are you not overly dressed, Dad?" he asked.

"No time to change, we got home late

remember? We rushed right out of the house," Sgt. Silverstar replied.

"C.J. doesn't appear to be injured whatsoever," Nurse Silverstar said.

The Refs continued to pay attention to the action, allowing the game to play out.

"Boy, brutal, that's the way the cookie crumbles," Skylar said speaking in Murian idioms. "Enjoy being a ragdoll?" he asked.

"No." C.J. allowed this teammate closer to her, into her space bubble. She scanned the faces in the crowd searching for Chad and got a wave from Ernie, the genius.

"Who does your eye search for?" Skylar asked.

"Someone."

"Does this someone have a first, middle and last name?"

"Chad, silly."

"I saw him with Tammy, in his car, the same one that drove you both to the Queen-Knight Hockey Arena," Skylar replied deliberately telling the truth in a gentle tone of voice.

C.J.'s expression flushed with horror and shock.

Antiflick-Troopers' player 226 captured the puck and slapped another shot at the net.

Tiger-Girl used her body to block the shot, the padding providing excellent cover. And again the vulcanized disk ricocheted back into play.

A third Antiflick-Troopers' player slapped the puck hard at the net.

Tiger-Girl again blocked the aggressive attack.

The General wore jersey 437, so she became known as General-437, and played right defense. She had been born in Afghanistan and immigrated to Canada with her family at the age of four. The winter sport became her method of escapism.

She knew from reading the occasional newspaper, that once again in 2044, war and rage brewed in her homeland of Afghanistan under threat of warrior religious zealots. It was sheer horror and madness. Men never seemed to learn violence only inflamed hatred and women were often the scape goat. Anyway, her parents, both of them teachers and living safely in Canada, thousands of kilometers away from Afghanistan, encouraged their daughter to pick a sport and ba-boom in just a few years General-437 got handpicked from Queen-Knight scout Wild-Owl Butterscotch at the tender age of eight to become a member of the town team financed by the Atlas Corporation Hockeynomics Division.

Maneuvering up the rink on the right, General-437, while her parents watched from the bleachers, slipped between Antiflick-Troopers like a stealth aircraft. She snagged the vulcanize rubber disk away from her opponent commenting, "I will take that now," And she was gone. On the other hand, the opponent did not even notice until he went to make a slap on net, hoping to score. But he slipped, losing control of his stick and simultaneously fell on his butt. The L shaped stick went flying away in another direction.

Some hockey fans laughed at this situation calling out: "Open your eyes", "Are you for real, kid?", "Get a pair of glasses ding-bat!" Looking around dazed and confused, he wondered where the puck was.

Meanwhile, General-437 spun around in the opposite direction and like a tank she ploughed through three approaching opponents and they fell, *splat!*

The Hindu ref blew the whistle stopping the action.

Bummer!

The ref made a gesture indicating General-437 was charging, an offence in the sport, and had caused the three Antiflick-Troopers to lose their balance. It was as though they were the Three Stooges wearing skates.

"This is absurd!" C.J. cursed, looking at Skylar.

"Hey, you two, get with the game!" a fan shouted out.

Eighteen-year-old Captain Determination skated over as it was her duty, bearing jersey number 401 with the stitched on letter C. Taking off her helmet, she revealed her beautiful oval black face and Cleopatra hair style.

"Why didn't you call the play against C.J.?" she asked suspiciously, squaring-off with the Short Official with her hands resting on her hips.

"C.J. and Skylar are over there doing fine!" the short ref rebutted.

"Fazillah, you charged three Antiflick-Troopers, I am giving you a warning not to be so aggressive," the Hindu ref said.

"Bull," General-437 replied. "I snatched the puck and made an evasive action. If these bozos cannot stand on blades of steel, that isn't my issue, nor should I be penalized for it," she spoke emphatically, gesturing to the trio of Antiflick-Troopers struggling to get up. "They remind me of the Vaudeville Canadian 1940s comedy team, the Mixed-Nuts."

"Mixed-Nuts? Learn to shut off the TV, you weren't even born in the 1940s Fazillah!" the Hindu ref scolded.

"But I have seen old 1940s black and white films on Metroburb TV station, channel 69," General-437 replied.

"Sir," Captain Determination said speaking up calmly, "the Antiflick-Troopers were bullying my teammate."

C.J. and Skylar joined in the situation and then it got into a serious debate of overlapping conversations.

Christina "Chrissy" Tereshkova skated over to the group. And Chrissy's oval opaque eyes reflected the image of people making other people uncomfortable. Chrissy mutated her eyes to resemble a human pair.

"I saw who dunnit," she admitted.

"I saw the whole thing too" C.J. repeated and took off her helmet.

"I also was a witness," Skylar said pointing to a player wearing a green helmet.

"Stop lying, C.J.," the short official rebutted.

"Prove I did not witness what happened." C.J. crossed her arms irked. "You make a foul call on General-437, but never called foul against the Antiflick-Trooper for slamming me against the boards. Shame on you!"

Skylar was being ignored.

"Which player hit you against the boards, C.J.? Point this player out!" the short ref asked.

In her mind something tingled, one Antiflick-Trooper was guilty, but which face looked guilty enough to point a finger at. Tiny vibrations deep in her mind sensed various minds within a twenty-five meter range. "My best guess is jersey two-two-three," C.J. replied.

"It wasn't me!" the Antiflick-Trooper player said in an innocent voice. "My name is Britney Sasquatch. This finger pointing is crap. I am a First Nations person of Canada, and I know the rules about roughing in the Atlas Hockey co-ed Hockey League. This is all I have ever wanted to do other than be a reporter. My news website back home in Antiflick is

Sasquatch@News. I send news tips into the Saskacity-Burb Newspaper and have even gotten published. And although we are considered by the NHL as a globetrotting freaks; this is my freaky sport and I don't consider myself a freak of nature. And my parents both work in at the Canadian Mackenzie Industrial Space Centre just outside Saskacity. My father designs Canada's advance aircraft and including vehicles for Mars. All of you are aware the Atlas Corporation in conjunction with other earth space agencies established a colony of three thousand humans on Mars since touchdown 2020," she said speaking quickly and shook C.J.'s hand in an exaggerated way.

C.J. giggled at how the girl spoke, what did any of that have to do with the situation at hand? Britney reminded her Ernie. Okay, she was wrong this time.

"C.J., it wasn't me!" Britney insisted, but she did wear a green helmet.

"C.J., I witnessed who smashed you against the boards," Chrissy spoke up tugging on the jersey sleeve, but was also ignored.

Queen-Knight player 407, Sergio, curiously skated over to the situation followed by his Murian teammate Zack, in jersey 415.

"We are not engaging in a meeting of the minds like those big wigs at the United Nations," the short ref spoke up.

The Hindu ref looked flustered, "I will

subtract the warning this time, Fazillah."

C.J. interrupted boldly, "Hey, pal, that's General number four-three-seven."

"Grow up," the short ref insisted, "going around lying as you do will not earn you any brownie points. I wonder how much you lie to your parents."

C.J. cast an expression at the ref and then towards Captain Determination, a girlfriend who had become a good friend, a sister. She proved her worth to her at a Halloween party at fourteen.

Captain Determination spoke up, "Ref, C.J. got washed against the boards a few minutes ago, so why was the player not penalized?"

"I don't need to discuss my rulings with you Captain," the Hindu ref replied.

Captain Determination focussed her attention at the ref feeling an invisible punch. "Fortunately my best player did not receive injuries, but your game actions as a ref will be called into account."

"Is that a threat?"

"My father is an RMCP detective and my family is watching this ACHL game. You are being informed under Chapter two, paragraph four in the ACHL rulebook, that as a hockey player in the co-ed sport, I have the right to challenge your ruling," Captain Determination said with full intensity. "You burned C.J., my best player."

"We will have a face-off. Get into your play positions," the Hindu ref said, "Captain I made an honest mistake. Every decision I make I am trying very hard to do the right thing. This is the last game of regular season."

"Thank you for admitting it."

The players got into position.

A moment later an Antiflick-Trooper player bumped C.J.

"Britney didn't hit you, it was me," Antiflick-Trooper 229 confessed whispering into C.J.'s ear. "Revenge for the last game when you tripped me with your stick and the refs did not call the play. You may call me, Bear-Sister, my official Murian name, and you'd better watch your back!"

C.J. jerked her head around so she could see the face of the Antiflick-Trooper through the protective helmet. The girl smirked. She had a human face, but then she mutated and it became a Murian face with oval opaque eyes and whiskers of a cat. Bear-Sister wanted to disguise herself, to blend in and look ordinary. After a split second, through supernatural powers, the girl shifted her facial features to again resemble a Sumerian. She skated away.

As much as C.J. wanted to go straight into a fight, she knew the Murian girl could muster supernatural powers. She too possessed something unique, but kept it a secret. Would she be able to fight a Murian and win? C.J. relaxed her fists because an idea popped into her mind how to adapt this situation to her favour.

The puck got dropped at centre ice.

YOU REALLY INTERROGATE ME

"It's Saturday morning on the 22nd of April, and it was already unseasonably warm. By 6:23 it had already reached a high of 25 degrees on the Metroburb humidity index," the Metro-Zoom radio station OMG personality spoke on C.J.'s laptop. "And, congratulations for you folks living in the town of Queen-Knight; the ACHL co-ed hockey team beat the Antiflick-Troopers."

C.J. checked the weather status on Metro-Zoom information and then closed the laptop. Next, she opened the door of the apartment located on the top floor of the four storey Valkyrie estate, located on Arrow Road in the town of Queen-Knight.

C.J. decided to exit the apartment through the side door, and jogged down the switchback steel stairwell which had a grip floor designed for winter requirements. A fireman's pole had recently been installed just in case. The apartment was there for the renting, but instead of someone from outside the family, C.J. took it over and paid a small fee for rent.

As C.J. reached the driveway with the five garage doors, a copper tone Thor car pulled out. Thors were manufactured by the Stronach Automotive Conglomerate and it produced several all Canadian vehicles, including the Sauropod.

"Flying today, C.J.?" RCMP Sgt. Silverstar asked lowering the tinted window.

"It's Saturday, I fly like a bird on Sundays, long weekends or holidays," she reminded him while jogging on the spot, "you should know my Saturday routine. Saturday I jog with Robyn."

RCMP Sgt. Silverstar interrupted, "Robyn; that Murian has an RCMP record extending back to the late 1940s and 1950s as a teenager."

"Robyn is in no way a criminal mastermind, Dad!" C.J. launched in a verbal defense.

"A deterioration of moral discipline is a virus a few Murians suffer from like lead foot syndrome. Anyway, three hundred and sixteen live in the Supermax in Saskacity."

"Skylar told me, for your information, Daddy-o; an estimated eight thousand Murians are imprisoned for various bullock offences."

"No need for colourful poetry of words."

C.J. balked. "Tell me as an RCMP sergeant that you don't use colourful poetry!"

"When and where it is necessary." He smirked in a cheesy manner.

"Self-righteousness!" C.J. scolded, pausing from jogging on the spot.

"I am practical in life."

"The Murian you speak so low of is my trainer, and we often exercise together at Queen-Knight Gym. God, I wish you would let up on me choosing friends," C.J. argued.

"Hmm," RCMP Sgt. Silverstar commented.

"I juggle working at the Valkyrie Hotel, and

homework, playing hockey, which gets me up as early as five a.m., and sometimes I don't get to return home till eight in the morning. Coach Candice occasionally will set up a scrimmage game verse the all-boys' team, the Thunder-Screamers, where Chad is the captain, and they can go on all night."

"Hmm."

"Dad, you sound intolerant of Murians. You aren't, are you?" C.J. asked suspiciously. "What if I started dating Skylar?"

"I might be...presumptuous about Robyn," RCMP Sgt. Silverstar said selecting his words carefully. "I would immediately approve of Skylar, his parents are employed through H.O.C.K.E.Y."

"You didn't arrest Chad for kissing me after the Queen-Knights won the game, that was sweet," C.J. said.

"Question: would you use your computer to hack into my RCMP laptop to view police files?" he asked sternly.

"Why on earth would I want to read about girls being stalked by crazed boyfriends or the arrest of some moron who has veins full of some toxic chemical? I have better activities to do, Daddy-o," C.J. said, continuing in their typical punchy relationship, "Your files have pictures of blood splattered crime scenes. Need I say more?"

RCMP Sgt. Silverstar smiled. He pulled a cellphone out of his breast pocket. "I was recording this conversation for quality and control purposes and

I will take it back to the forensic lab to have it analyzed," he said.

"Dad, you really interrogated me?"

"I am RCMP, that's my job, C.J.," he said, "And congratulations for scoring back to back against the Antiflick-Troopers last night. Your mother, Ernie, and I were concerned when you got hit during the game. I am unsure how you survived that blow and bounced back so quickly," RCMP Sgt. Silverstar said.

"Superheroes can regenerate," C.J. teased. Next, she shrugged. "At least one of the two refs should have called a penalty against the Antiflick-Trooper."

"You really want me to demonstrate what an interrogation is?"

"I was joking!"

"Officer Grant texted me about the regular donations you're making because of your lead foot syndrome," RCMP Sgt. Silverstar said, "and she has an envelope with each of your one hundred dollar bills."

C.J. flushed an expression of total surprise. "What? Officer Grant has saved all that money, I – I don't know what you're implying!"

"C.J.!" RCMP Sgt. Silverstar barked. "You are my daughter." He got out, standing clearly taller and as a man of the law, more muscular. "C.J., strictly speaking, this is in the family, your actions are understood, however by law your actions can be considered a bribe. You do not bribe a police officer."

C.J. felt her throat tighten. This was the first time her father ever confronted her like this, standing one inch away intruding on her personal space. She shivered.

"Daddy… Please… You are frightening me."

"Daddy? You are not a child, you are eighteen. Your mother and I decided we would raise you and your brother in the real world."

C.J. nodded.

"You earn a wage playing in the ACHL co-ed sport of hockey, plus part time hours at the family Valkyrie Hotel as a waitress, so maybe you feel like spreading the wealth?" RCMP Sgt. Silverstar asked.

"Yeah," C.J. stretched the word.

"Speak English. Yes: the word is YES. Yes, you are spreading the wealth," RCMP Sgt. Silverstar said.

"Mom allowed me to withdraw money from my trust fund on my birthday, remember."

"How much?"

"Five."

"Five thousand, whew, toward university, right?" RCMP Sgt. Silverstar asked.

"No, it wasn't that much," C.J. said and laughed transforming back to her punchy style.

"How much, Five hundred thousand?"

"A girl cannot live on five hundred thousand in 2045, try five million." C.J. had a no nonsense expression.

Silence fell.

"Five million? Kids these days," RCMP Sgt. Silverstar muttered.

"My trust fund is at one hundred million dollars, thanks to my very rich uncles and so mom told me I could withdraw up to five million so I, you know, can do things and be relaxed. I am going to university," C.J. said.

"Five million." RCMP Sgt. Silverstar repeated bewildered and shocked. He got back inside the car.

"You seemed taken by surprise, Dad. Five million these days isn't really a whole lot of money: milk is up to five dollars per liter, charging my all-electric Sauropod is twenty-five cents every five minutes, going to a hologram movie is expensive, fifty dollars for a single ticket. I pay you and mom rent for my place to be responsible, that's twenty-five hundred per month: and maybe because I am living at home you and mom are giving me a real economic break. I am educated enough to understand what goes on in this complex world we live in, Daddy-o."

"How many cheese burgers does Chad need to eat?" RCMP Sgt. Silverstar asked.

"I am sorry about bribing Officer Grant. That was wrong of me."

"The question is C.J., what will you do with that money? A lot of money can corrupt people. My own family is part of the military industries, but when I withdrew money, I took enough, but never five million. The Valkyrie family possesses a vast ocean of currency. Money breeds corruption."

"Are you afraid I will become a criminal?" C.J. accused. "I live in your home and the secrets I possess I will keep close to my heart because they are important to me. I won't disappoint you, Daddy-o."

Silence came again.

"I have unfinished reports on the mutts'," RCMP Sgt. said, "I Got a message on my RCMP phone about a prison break in Saskacity. H.O.C.K.E.Y. is on it. Two dangerous Murians I guess want to try their luck again. Kate is in Britannia with Susan's mom, and Ernie, your wanna-be Martian astronaut brother, will be doing whatever my son does on his Saturdays. Ahem," he cleared his throat playful way, "I haven't interrogated him this morning."

"Go easy on, Ernie, he is my brother!" C.J. deliberately pretended to gag herself. "He is so smart he makes smart people look like dolts, the next super brain on planet earth."

"Takes after his old man!" RCMP Sgt. Silverstar said gesturing with two-thumbs-up and laughed at his own joke. He drove away down the kilometer long lane and the iron gate's electronic red-eye spied the vehicle approaching and opened automatically.

THE ENCLAVE

C.J. opened a two inch thick iron door next to a sliding gate after using a plastic coded key to get outside. Next, she tucked it inside a side pocket on her knee-length sports gear designed for the athletic woman. It followed the contours of her hockey-built body. These types of clothes kept her cool because it was breathable so any type of sweat would be reduced and kept skin free of irritation. The pants were designed to be stretchable in four-ways so she could perform a multitude of exercises comfortably. Chad had considered her to be pin-up material when clad in this outfit. He had printed off a picture of her on his computer, enlarging it, and had taped it on his bedroom wall. When she saw it after being invited over one afternoon to help Chad with homework, she guffawed, but at his request she autographed it for him. If other guys did not consider C.J. pin-up material, that was their delusional issue.

C.J. wired herself up to her earphones and then tapped the single glowing clock-button turning on the super slim all-Canadian device. It was only five millimetres thick. The glowing clock-button faded away and the control surface became ebony. The first song blasting through the small ear-speakers was her favourite by the twentieth century singer, Tina Turner, *Simply the Best*. She had gotten the song from Queen-Knight Captain Determination, or Susan.

She had introduced her to the song and the rest had become history. This had all been a month or so after protecting Susan from sexual assault during a Halloween party.

C.J. figured Susan used to bully her because she felt threatened. She must have thought *here comes some white chick who could easily take away my opportunity to be the captain of the hockey team.* It took Susan a while to realize C.J. thoroughly enjoyed playing co-ed hockey, but also had other hopes and dreams. "Hockey is just one thing I enjoy, I also enjoy flying my Cessna, Silver-Bird. Let me take you into the sky," she invited Susan. At age of seventeen she could fly solo with the same skill of a sparrow pilot, performing rollover maneuvers and turning the plane upside down. "Tell you a secret, Susan, I applied to the Sparrow Flying Aces School for advanced aerial acrobatics, and if I ever got the opportunity to take eight weeks of summer to learn more tricks of the trade, I would have to give up hockey."

Bright sunshine bathed Arrow Road in an enchanting way. The sun sat at the end of the street seemed as if it was cosmically connected to the rising star over the distant horizon.

Garbage collectors moved along Arrow Road using wireless robot droids to pick up trashcans and dump them inside the back of the truck. This was possible because the town of Queen-Knight, just like the cities of Metroburb, Saskacity, Britannia,

Quebec's Champlain City and Alberta's Cold-City; were twenty-first century smart-towns.

Eight eighty foot towers surrounded Queen-Knight with dozens of antennae that fanned out and through a wireless system that maintained an electric grid over the town. This enabled garbage collectors to control the droids far better than even fifteen years ago. Queen-Knight competed on the same smart system as selected towns across Europe and Great Britain.

C.J. met up with Robyn Tundra in much the same way they always met up, while jogging. *Whoosh.* The Murian woman arrived next to her coming out of a burst of speed and slowed down to a comfortable jogging pace. She knew Robyn had competed in six Murian Olympics that demonstrated one of her supernatural abilities, speed. She was able to break two hundred and fifty kilometers per hour. Robyn had competed in the five hundred kilometer relay race along the Trans-Canada Highway in 2035 against an American team of Murians. She won gold, but just how fast Robyn could run, C.J. did not know. What other supernatural abilities Robyn possessed was classified by Canadian Murian Law Title 808.

"Congratulations for winning the hockey game," she said while jogging. "I saw the highlights broadcasted on the town's exterior big screen TV. The Queen-Knights will first face the NHL Stanley Cup winners of last season in Hockey City, and then zoom off to Europe to Murian Island.

Congratulations."

"Team effort," C.J. replied without being winded, just as any physically fit young woman should be able to carry a conversation while jogging. Together they went along Arrow Road for three kilometers and passed a sign which read in bold letters:

WELCOME TO THE MURIAN ENCLAVE
POP. 15, 317

They continued along Arrow Road approaching the top of Steep Hill, as the residents had nicknamed it. From there, they could oversee the valley of farms with houses dating back to the 1800s. A few wells were still operational. The population of the modern era demanded the construction of two apartment super complexes, but no more were scheduled for construction until well into the twenty-second or perhaps even as far down the road as the twenty-third century. The Murian Council insisted on keeping the enclave reasonably free of construction as much as possible, and many of the residents also wanted it that way. Some had opposed the construction of the two super complexes, but demand for living space within the enclave by the younger boom generation of Murians overruled their issues. Only Arrow Road was paved, all roads extended off left or right were unpaved.

The Murian baby boom had occurred in the

late 1970s when the Canadian Government gave the Canadian First World Race, or supernatural race, the right to procreate without the need of asking permission as many other nations had insisted. Some had created laws to keep their population under two offspring. Considering that the lifespan of an average Murian was eight times longer than a Sumerian, the new generation of Murians were now young adults and they now had offspring. For whatever reason, they had agreed with the Canadian Government to keep their families under three offspring. The Canadian Government thought it was absurd for a man and a woman in modern times to need a license just to have kids, although many other countries had insisted, including the U.S.A.

Besides, the Canadian Government since 2025, had opened a window of thirty years for only white Canadian couples to procreate to increase the white population. This had become necessary considering the last of the creed was now the senior citizen population of 1944-1945, which were dying out and or dead. The government had offered three thousand dollars per year for any white families to have five, to as many as seven offspring, within that thirty year period. However, there were rules to the game that included resettling in the prairies to increase the white population out there, Ontario and Quebec were barred from playing along.

By 2045, fifteen thousand Canadian families, including families from the eastern side of Canada;

Newfoundland, P.E.I. and New Brunswick, who had taken part, had helped increase the population. It was like going back in time when prairies required settlements and land was cheap. Many of the white families had achieved five offspring and some had managed as many as nine.

The controversial "Baby-Maker Bill" as dubbed by an American media empire, scolded parliament for disallowing black Canadian families who had dwelled in the country with an ancestry going as far back as 1867 to breed. It had been challenged in court, and allowed a handful of black Canadians to participate, though not as many as one would like. There was no shortage of wrangling at any time in parliament.

At the top of Steep Hill, C.J. could see to the right an off lime coloured mound similar in size to the famous Australian copper-red mound. The enclave was a town surrounded by a larger town, and the fourth largest settlement of Murians outside of the Alberta and British Columbian zones. The others consisted of Murian Island in the North Sea, as well another enclave in Europe.

Robyn Tundra was born in 1925, but resembled a woman of only forty-eight due to the Murian aging process. A Sumerian woman born then would be one hundred and twenty and dead by 2045. Poor Robyn had no offspring because her uterus was deformed. She currently lived with a Sumerian man, her second husband that was into taking care of his body, a gym teacher at Queen-Knight High School. Her first Sumerian husband had been another Canadian Olympic athlete who had won the gold in the one hundred meter dash. He had set a world record running the race in eight seconds flat. She had two adopted kids, one Murian and one Sumerian from her first marriage, and they were now adults with families of their own. She kept in contact with them. She would outlive her own Sumerian child.

"Are you planning to take a walk through Britannia?"

"Why do ask?" C.J. asked suddenly being defensive. She smoothly side stepped a pile of horse manure. "Whew! Big land mine."

Robyn laughed. "Icky, land mines are a regular feature within the Murian Enclave."

They continued to jog at a casual pace.

"In the Queen-Knight Newspaper there is an intriguing article on page six," Robyn commented.

"The mysterious Street Surgeon cannot do everything. They protect the homeless from roughneck groups like the Street Hood, Thug and Gang-Up," C.J. replied as she approached the halfway mark of Steep Hill that was marked by an off-coloured lime boulder. "This person, the Street Surgeon, has been sited within Ebony-Shine over fifteen hundred times since the 1980s. I downloaded five hundred articles from a small website: Sasquatch@News before I got cut off by someone operating the website. I got an email sixty seconds later informing me that it costs money to obtain the articles and was told to pay one hundred and fifty dollars for the five hundred articles, bummer. Anyway, the first recorded sighting of the Street Surgeon was in May 1980. And my RCMP Sgt. father has a dossier a quarter of an inch thick complete with fuzzy black and white photos taken from various security cameras. Eight sightings that occurred in Ebony-Shine took place this year, in March 2045, and the Street Surgeon eluded a team of an undercover officers similar to the way a Murian using supernatural powers would be able to do. I am pretty sure my Father is in charge of the investigation. I asked my little brother to hack into his computer using my laptop. Ernie promised he would not tell, and as a deal I bought him a summer pass to the Canadian Hockey theme park," C.J. said. She casually looked into the azure-sky and overhead flew a flock of Canadian sparrow hypersonic jets. "I applied to the sparrow aerospace program as a back-up plan in case my hockey career melts," she added.

"Ebony-Shine?" Robyn repeated the word.

"The homeless call it Ebony-Shine. It's where darkness shines brighter than the sun," C.J. explained, "and I know of this because an article I downloaded from Sasquatch@News claims a million homeless people are being held hostage by five powerful corporations known as the Ring-of-Fire, something like that anyway. The news reporter is nicknamed Sasquatch and she claims her family once resided in the region that is now Britannia, or Ebony-Shine. As I said, I prefer Ebony-Shine. Sasquatch claims that her family, who are First Nation Canadians, made canoes for the Canoe Clan family. The alleyways of Ebony-Shine to me are designed like a maze. The alleyways go in one direction and suddenly become dead ends and they go left and right, zigzag about. In one peculiar zone there is a shanty suburb where people live. Some people dwell in various sized tents. Tent City: that's what the Street Nation calls it."

"Britannia was once a beautiful city. I was born, as you are aware, in 1925. Murians don't age as rapidly as Sumerians, but we are also capable of being killed by something as simple as a lead projectile. Some Murians can regenerate and survive the stings of an ugly bullet. My parents were killed in Britannia one night by a group of religious people. They fought to stop a single man, Dr. Methopolis from waging a secret street war against the people dwelling within Britannia during the 1940s and 50s. And so I lived on the streets into my early twenties, surviving. I too belonged to a street group, the Wildcards, before a Murian family adopted me and moved out of the city during the 1950s, and invited me to the Murian Enclave. I felt happy for the first time. I had a family again. I went by a different name back in the day," Robyn commented revealing something about her life she preferred to keep a secret. Perhaps the secret should remain unknown, but she felt it important to share it with her young

Sumerian friend.

C.J. half listened to Robyn, but was concentrating on other things. "I also like hockey," C.J. insisted, carrying on the conversation from her thoughts. "I am not a heroine seeking glory. I like helping others too, with whatever god gave me. Hockey is the best way of releasing my energy in a positive manner. I encourage young girls to participate, so I share my time with Girl Guides too. The Queen-Knights are playing the NHL Saskacity Hercules Stanley Cup winners at Hockey City." C.J.'s mind repeated the conversation from an hour and half ago. *"I applied to the Sparrow aerospace program as a back-up plan in case my hockey career melts,"* she looked to the sky and added, "Those hypersonic jets must be returning to Saskacity, to Area 49 a.k.a. the Beehive."

"How do you feel?"

"Why do you ask?" C.J. inquired without being defensive.

"Since your accident during your nature walk at fourteen, you have demonstrated certain abilities, C.J.."

"My parents don't know about my incident in the forest that day during the field trip, Captain Determination knows, and Chrissy, my other Murian girl friend. I have told you about Chrissy. Her father is the Russian trillionaire industrialist. He has companies all over the world including the Beehive. Chad knows, and so does Fazillah," C.J. said.

"Well, all the right people know your super-duper secret," Robyn teased.

"My father would kill me if he ever knew I was anywhere near Ebony-Shine."

"Are you not afraid that one day your parents will discover your secret?"

"My mom works in Ebony-Shine as a Street Nurse along with Susan's mom. She works out of Mission-21, the first and only medical facility run by Dr. Reece," C.J. said adding with a hush-hush tone of voice, "And it is financially backed by the Atlas Corporation, the one hundred trillion dollar corporation." She released a laugh. "Atlas Corporation is the eldest on earth with a history extending back to the Murians. From even before the artic island nation sank and the artic became a freezing landscape," she said.

"C.J., all secrets will eventually be learned one day. Our Murian Bible teaches that nothing stays a secret forever and therefore you cannot stay a secret forever."

"Is there divine intervention in this world?" She blurted the question and then covered her mouth as if hoping to keep that question a secret.

"I have two step-siblings that work for H.O.C.K.E.Y., and their Murian abilities are more than a match for even little ol' me," Robyn commented. "My older step-sister is Madusa. She wields the ability transform anyone flesh, animal or human being, into crystal, and while in that state a person doesn't age. Only Madusa can undo the effect. But she can also harness other mental powers such as aerokenisis, no telekinesis that I am aware of, but some telepathy. Most Murians possess a little telepathy. Madusa has been trained in hand-to-hand combat skills while attending the Diefenbaker Complex. And never mind about my older step-brother, Winter-Giant," she said and released a girlish giggle.

"Supernatural powers, I am intrigued," C.J. commented.

"I have never told anyone so much information, C.J., so you are bringing out the fun in me today!" Robyn gave a hug to her young friend. She would never reveal the H.O.C.K.E.Y. code names. If it wasn't for them, things in her life would be extremely different.

"Do you believe in divine intervention?" C.J. asked.

"To answer your question about divine intervention, our two genomes are three percent different when comparing Sumerians to Murians." She paused for a moment in thought adding, "the Sumerian genome is three percent different from the ape. Scientists use the words mortal or human: divine intervention is nature's response to human folly."

C.J. stopped jogging and Robyn followed suit. C.J. scratched her head puzzled by the comment, "I am Sumerian. Why would nature respond back to us?"

"Your accident during the nature walk, during the school fieldtrip to the Metroburb Science Centre," Robyn said, "you told me you came into contact with something extraordinary. Did you experience and alien abduction, C.J.?" she asked bluntly.

C.J.'s expression twisted. Did she have an experience with something out of this world?

"As a Murian, I believe earth is a living breathing organism because my people have lived on earth for tens of thousands of years, even before the birth and death of the Atlantean Race. Murians are the First World Nation. Our genome is connected to the mysterious Leylines surrounding the earth. It gives us our supernatural abilities. This is why our appendages work differently than in Sumerian anatomy. Our procreators, the Annunaki, developed us to be connected to the environment around us. But as a Sumerian, you should not possess the type of powers you do. However, you do, and thus nature is responding back to your people. I believe there is some divine intervention, there must be and it my guess is that it is the earth."

"Yes," C.J. blurted understanding a little bit. "What am I saying "yes" to?"

Robyn rested her hands on C.J.'s shoulder countering. "Would you like to race me at your top speed?"

"Is that a challenge?" C.J. asked in a competitive tone of voice.

"Most definitely. To the Murian Town Hall,

you should be able to handle a mere five kilometers."

C.J. exploded into a sprint kicking up a dust trail.

"Totally extreme this kid," Robyn muttered to herself adding. "C.J. must be running at one hundred kilometers at least. Where does her power come from?" Robyn wondered aloud. She suddenly leaped into a sprint from a standing position and followed.

The End of Volume One

Dear Superior Readers, Nerds & Nerdetts,

I hope you have enjoyed reading the first volume of *C.J. Silverstar*. In the sequel, *Extreme Metal Machine*, mysterious hammers rain down upon Parallel Earth 2. C.J. and one of her supernatural friends, Chrissy, find one. Skylar Turnspeak also finds a hammer, but what is their importance? Learn much more about Dr. Methopolis and watch his power grow. Read as a twist about Robyn Tundra's roots is revealed. Take a peek at the Moonsteep solar system. The sequel has many oddball twists that will leave you breathless and wanting to read the third installment!

Sincerely,

Clayton Crawford

P.S. If you have enjoyed this installment of C.J. Silverstar, the biggest compliment you could give me would be to recommend this book to another person. Word of mouth is a powerful thing, please help to get my story out there.

Sneak Peak from C.J. Silverstar Volume 2

Saskacity
Founded 1850
Population 507, 270
The Beehive
Sunday

Saskacity sat close to Prince Albert National Park and close enough to three bodies of water; Montreal Lake, Little Red River, and Sturgeon Lake. It was a military city. One hundred and eighty thousand employees worked at the Canadian Mackenzie Atlas Silverstar Space Industries making it the single largest Canadian employer in current times. The employees simply nicknamed it the beehive. The Canadian Government designated the area for military use during the Parallel Earth War beginning in 1945 following the end of the second world war.

The famous winged seagusus and pegasus horses floating in the azure blue sky circled the area. They would release a vocal sound announcing their intention to the regular horses, and then tilt their wings in a manner akin to a pilot preparing to land. The wings manipulated the airflow becoming like those of a glider, but the horses gracefully used their wing muscles to continuously shift them. Soon they would land in a large exterior field and gallop one hundred yards the way a plane would in order to slow down. They would be soon grazing next to wild

Canadian mustangs. The Tower had spotters watching the pegasus and seagusus through binoculars. "Touchdown!" someone would say.

The Beehive's internal area was recognizable with three supersized warehouses containing highly advanced aerospace planes for astronauts.

One of the red and white triangle aerospace planes rolled out of a hanger, ready to go. A tow truck with an attached long pulling rig hefted the triangle aerospace plane to the lift zone adjacent the five kilometre landing strip. The driver did not move very quickly, in fact the pace was at a crawl as he was guided by three men co-ordinating the action. He was given the signal to stop.

Inside were eight new Canadian astronauts. They did not need to wear space suits like the old twentieth century astronauts, but instead wore comfortable space clothes. They each wore a helmet which included a chin mic. The helmets were a tool for listening to conversations between the Tower and the pilot.

"The sky is clear, you are ready to launch."

"Ten-four, Mother," the Pilot teased. "I am warming up the vertical lift engines."

The green lights appeared as holograms within a screen built into the main window. "Go for vertical lift," the Tower controller ordered.

One of the astronauts was writing on a tablet, communicating to various Canadian kids online who were on his real-time/real-world communication system.

The red and white aerospace jet suddenly lifted vertically, spewing frothy cappuccino-like energy against the vertical pad. It thundered skyward, accelerating up to Mach 3. Suddenly, a boost of power surged and the aerospace jet screamed forward accelerating to Mach 6, 7, 9, 12, then Mach 15!

Looking through one of the windows, a Canadian astronaut could see two objects shoot by in the blink of an eye. He knew two more aerospace planes were returning from the donut-shaped International Space Station (ISS), with crew for a long awaited vacation no doubt.

Simultaneously two red and white aerospace crafts appeared in the sky as gliders. One by one they landed on the twelve kilometer runway. Parachutes popped out to help to slow them down.

Meanwhile, thousands of kilometers away, in Ontario, Ernie sat in the spacious backyard which included a tennis court, a pool surrounded by marble tiles and a twisty slide, wooden chairs, a garden, and a nine foot groomed hedge. Although it was late April and unusually warm no doubt due to the greenhouse effect, his parents alerted the pool man to come over to make his routine inspection.

The cities of Metroburb and Toronto had already released two heat alerts in the first two weeks of April and encouraged the tail end of the original baby boom generation a.k.a. the first generation-X, to keep cool inside malls and air conditioned recreation centres.

Ernie sat at the picnic table accompanied by friends and the blonde girl of fourteen, the one who had given him a kiss in the hall. They were all university kids set up in the Young Einstein Program at Queen-Knight University.

One of the kids was a Murian who demonstrated his supernatural ability of teleportation by disappearing from one spot in the backyard, only to reappear six feet above the pool. Unable to sustain a field of aerokenisis, he plopped into the water. The kids laughed. Quickly, the pool man helped the boy out, but he got pulled in, *splash!* The kids laughed harder. The Murian boy got a grip on his supernatural powers at last and rose up, holding the hand of the pool man who was kicking and screaming, "I can't swim! I can't swim!" The man was plopped on the lawn. The kids ran over to their friend, astonished.

"You saved his life!" The kids shared a hug and Ernie handed him a beach towel.

"Spoonleaf, you really need to work on your beaming,"

"Irregular thoughts scramble my mind, but you are as right as rain!"

The blonde eyed Spoonleaf then sized up Ernie. She thumped the air downward with both fists unsure of which one she now wanted to belong to. The redheaded girlfriend tapped her shoulder and whispered something that made her giggle.

The young men were ignoring the girls at this

moment in time, good chums, like fishing buddies. They talked about important young manly things, trading cards, comic books, movies, but not automobiles, not quite yet.

One boy had brought his guitar and strummed it playing imaginary tunes. He sat on a stool while wearing cool dark sunglasses, every inch a wanna-be rock n' roll legend.

"You sleep with that thing Fingers Charlie?" Ernie asked, calling his friend a nickname.

He replied with an Eastwood drawl, "Don't you sleep with your astronaut helmet, Mister Mars?"

"From time to time, instead of a nightlight," Ernie admitted. He suddenly got very excited. "Hey – Hey – I am online with astronaut Hatsmart!" And he gestured to his friends.

"What does this mean?" the green haired kid asked. Green had unnaturally green hair because he received daily injections of a formula for a patient with Leukemia. He could have as much life as any normal kid so long as he received 10ccs of an injection every day of his life. He earned the nickname, Mister Green.

"I am in conversation with an astronaut who is currently on rout to the ISS above the planet!" This was so cool to get real time conversations with a Canadian astronaut in 2045.

"What do you want to say?" the blonde girlfriend asked eagerly.

"Why don't you ask the question, Nancy," he

suggested sliding over the laptop.

"You mean that?" Nancy's eyes opened wide in surprise. She never expected Ernie to give her control of his laptop.

"You're cute, Ernie," Redhead blurted. Then, she got closer to Nancy and the two girlfriends watched the action on the laptop screen.

Street Nurse Silverstar stepped out of the living room at that moment, sliding across the transparent door adjacent the patio zone. She held two square boxes. She put them on the picnic table. Opening one box, the gang could see it contained peanut butter and jam, and marmalade sandwiches, and there was pepperoni with turkey, egg salad sandwiches, and small portion containers of potato salad. The sandwiches were cut into triangles. In another box were homemade baked chips, including dip. The name printed on the box read: **Valkyrie Hotel 24/7** restaurant services.

The kids began to gather around the food like a well hungry army.

A Murian man emerged from the house and placed a case of drinks on the picnic table. The label on the colds can read: Sodapop, by Methopolis Products.

"You young executives have been working hard, playing I bet, or getting ready to," the Murian Man said, "enjoy the food."

"You work with my Mom in Britannia?"

"Ernie, this is Mr. Cedar Chestnut-."

"This is my Dad," Spoonleaf interrupted.

"Son."

"I though you went to work today, Mom, isn't this Sunday?" Ernie suddenly smacked his palm against his forehead. "Duh!"

Nancy pulled his hand away in a defensive way. "Don't you dare smack yourself. You simply forgot what day it was, silly!"

"Ms. Silverstar," the pool man said standing at the edge of the pool, "it is okay to jump in and splash about," he added and then gave a smile at the kids. Suddenly he slipped and fell backwards into the pool releasing a yelp.

"He can't swim!" Ernie exclaimed. "Spoonleaf, do something!"

Mr. Chestnut outstretched his arms. He closed his eyes focussing his mind and then snatched the drenched pool man out of the water and dropped him on the lawn.

"Ernie, did you hack into the Beehive?" Street Nurse Silverstar asked, ignoring the pool-man.

"I am in conversation with astronaut Hatsmart, as he and his crew fly inside an aerospace scramjet to the ISS donut."